INSIDE... 2 AWESOME COMIC STRIPS

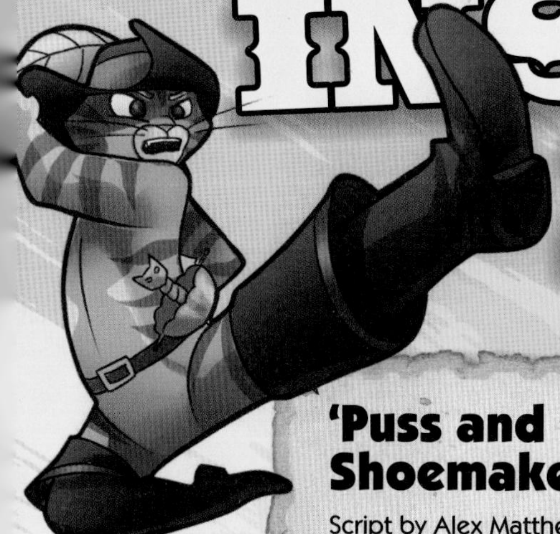

PLUS... 2 BONUS STORIES!!

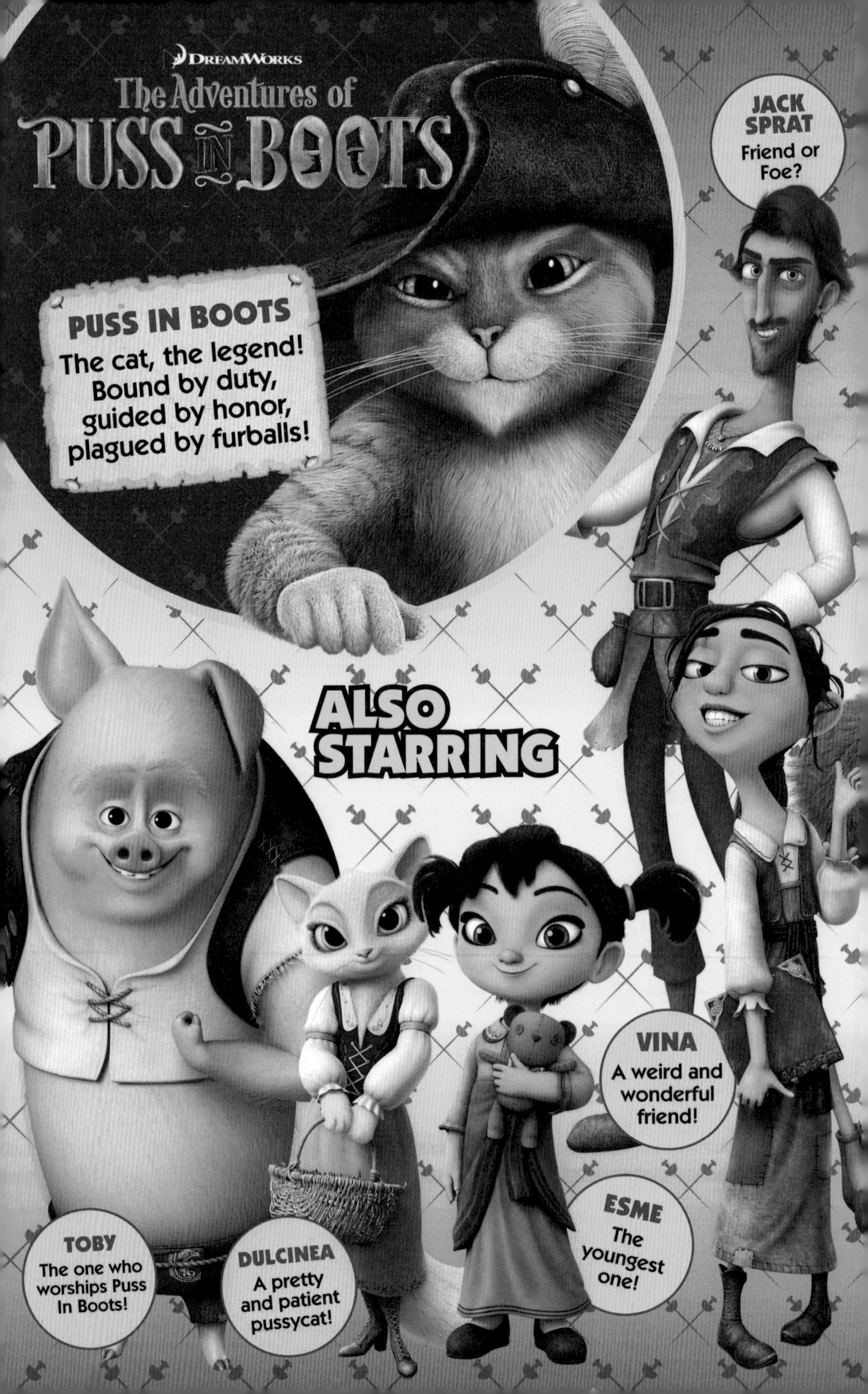
DreamWorks
The Adventures of
PUSS IN BOOTS
PUSS IN BOOTS
The cat, the legend! Bound by duty, guided by honor, plagued by furballs!
JACK SPRAT
Friend or Foe?
ALSO STARRING
VINA
A weird and wonderful friend!
ESME
The youngest one!
TOBY
The one who worships Puss In Boots!
DULCINEA
A pretty and patient pussycat!

DreamWorks

The Adventures of PUSS IN BOOTS

CAT ABOUT TOWN

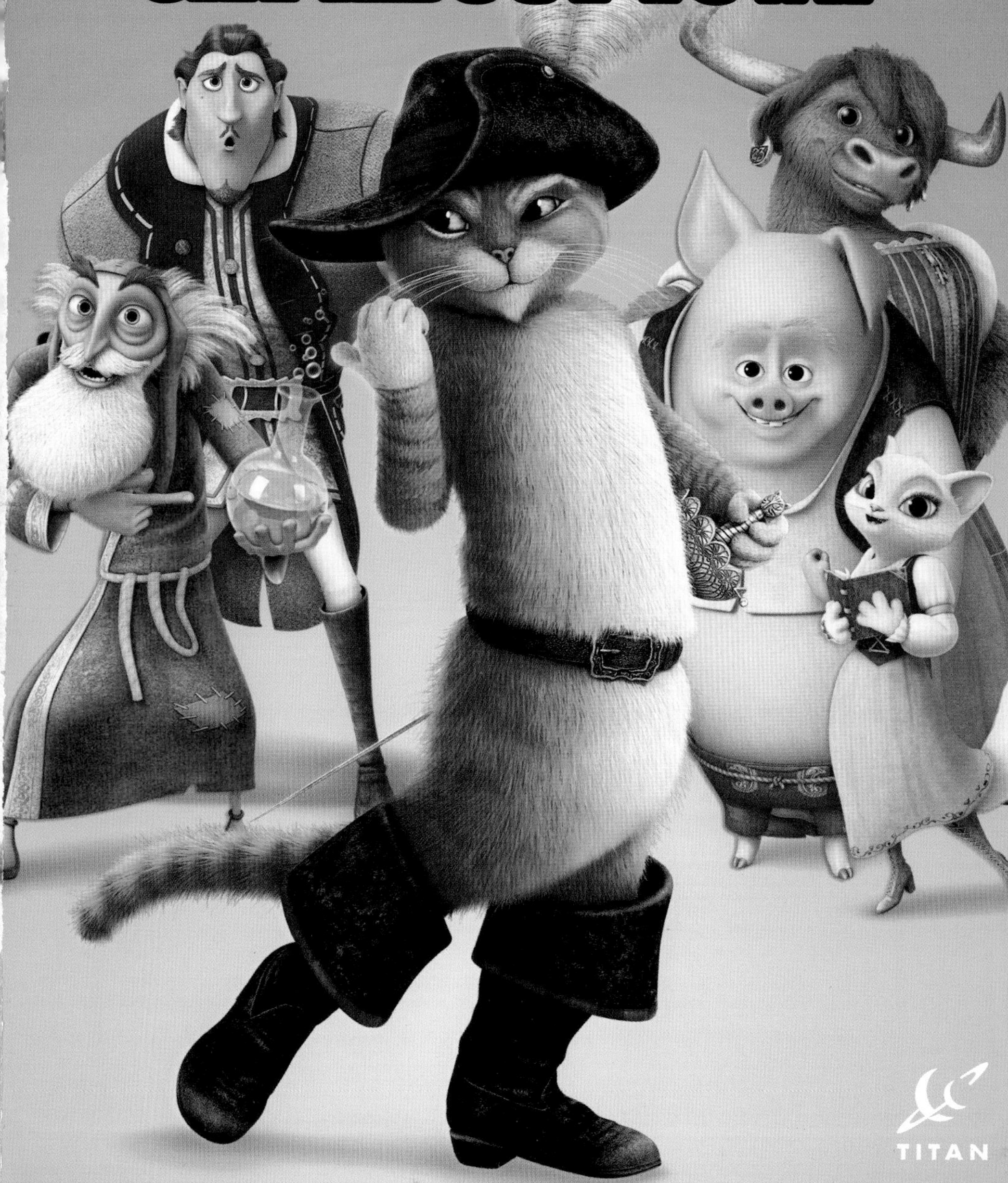

TITAN

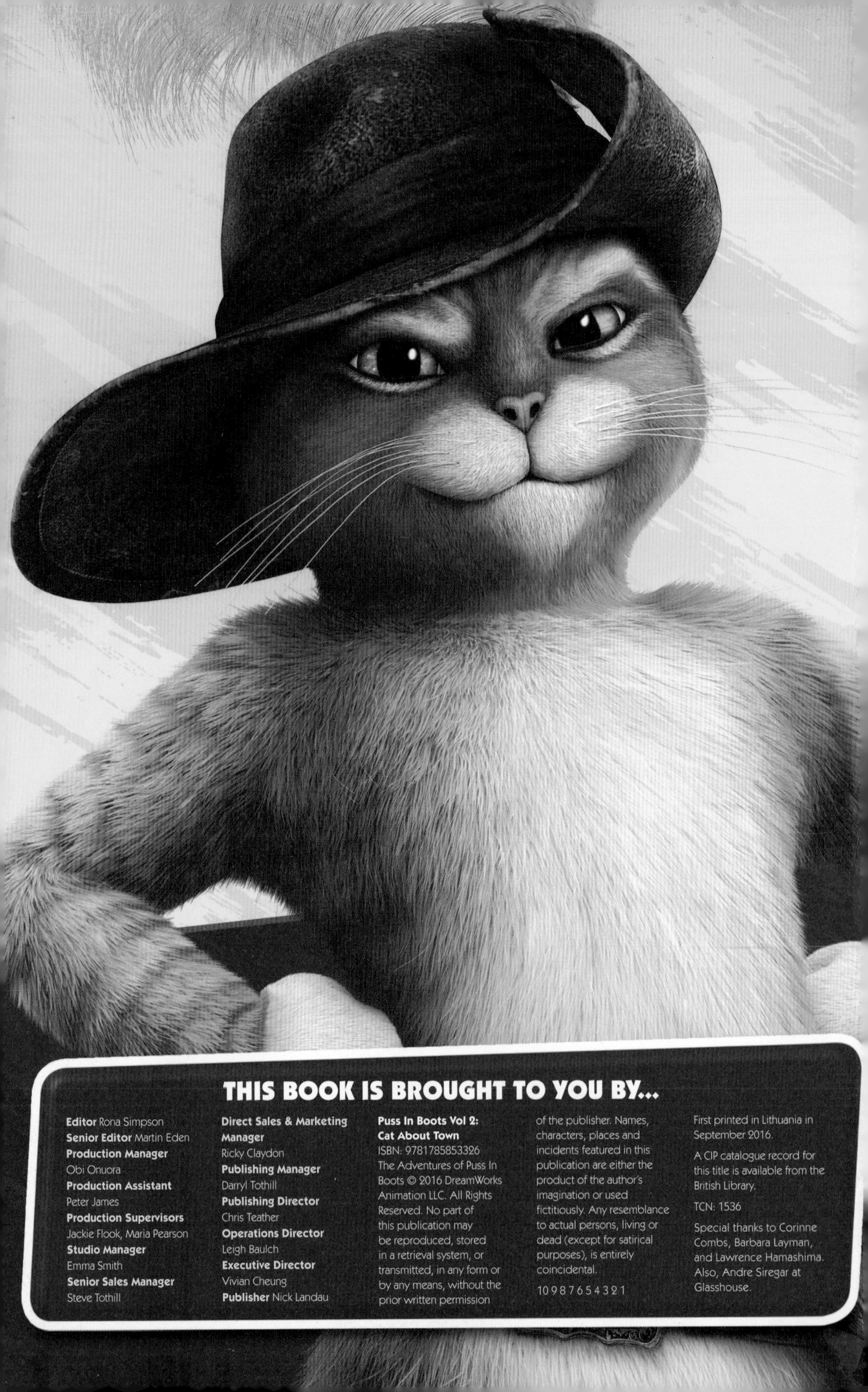

THIS BOOK IS BROUGHT TO YOU BY...

Editor Rona Simpson
Senior Editor Martin Eden
Production Manager Obi Onuora
Production Assistant Peter James
Production Supervisors Jackie Flook, Maria Pearson
Studio Manager Emma Smith
Senior Sales Manager Steve Tothill
Direct Sales & Marketing Manager Ricky Claydon
Publishing Manager Darryl Tothill
Publishing Director Chris Teather
Operations Director Leigh Baulch
Executive Director Vivian Cheung
Publisher Nick Landau

Puss In Boots Vol 2: Cat About Town
ISBN: 9781785853326

10 9 8 7 6 5 4 3 2 1

First printed in Lithuania in September 2016.

A CIP catalogue record for this title is available from the British Library.

TCN: 1536

Special thanks to Corinne Combs, Barbara Layman, and Lawrence Hamashima. Also, Andre Siregar at Glasshouse.

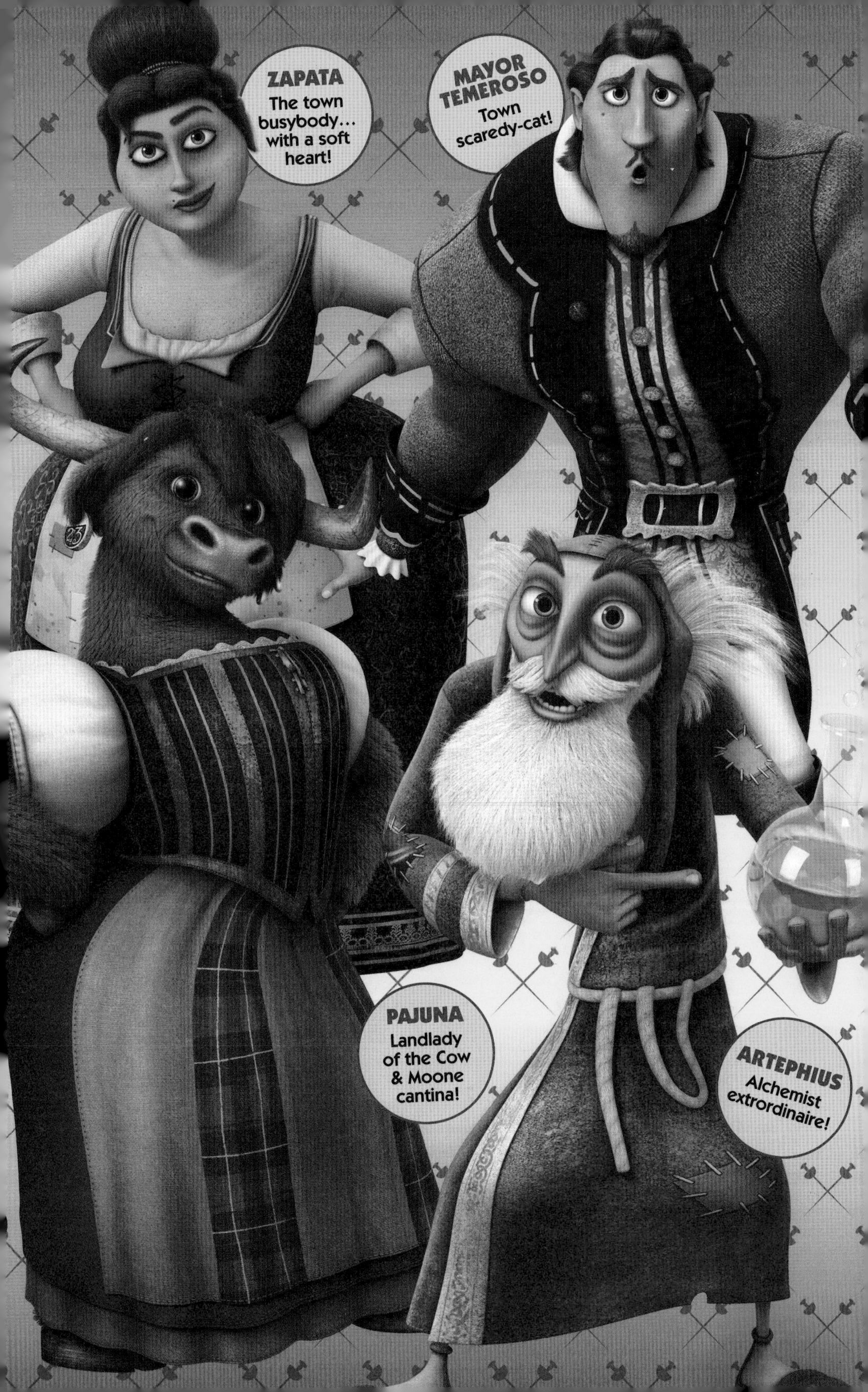
ZAPATA
The town busybody... with a soft heart!
MAYOR TEMEROSO
Town scaredy-cat!
PAJUNA
Landlady of the Cow & Moone cantina!
ARTEPHIUS
Alchemist extrordinaire!

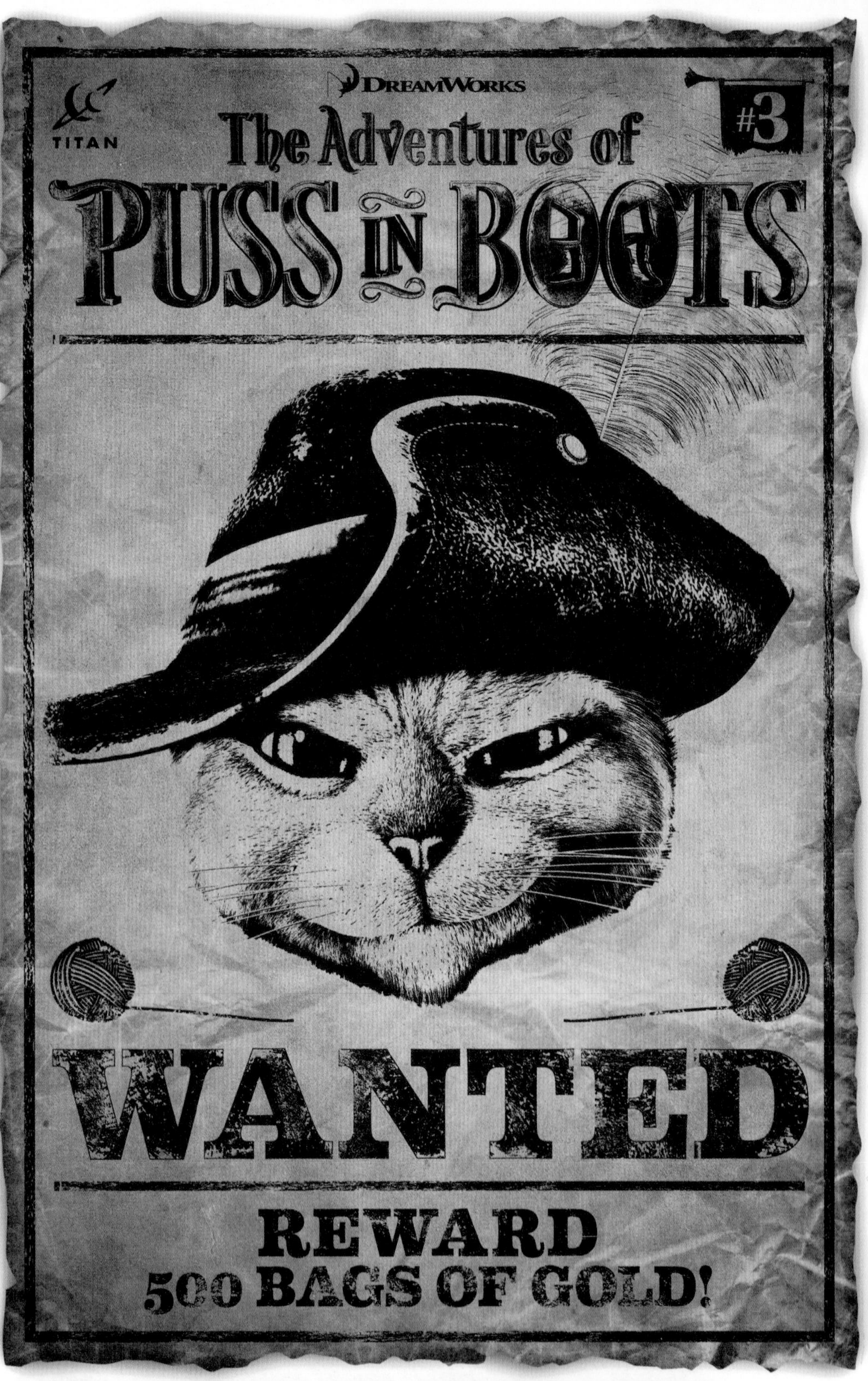
TITAN
DreamWorks
#3
The Adventures of
PUSS IN BOOTS
WANTED
REWARD
500 BAGS OF GOLD!

SCRIPT BY ALEX MATTHEWS • PENCILS BY EGLE BARTOLINI • INKS BY MARIA L SANAPO • COLORS BY KEVIN ENHART • LETTERING BY JIM CAMPBELL

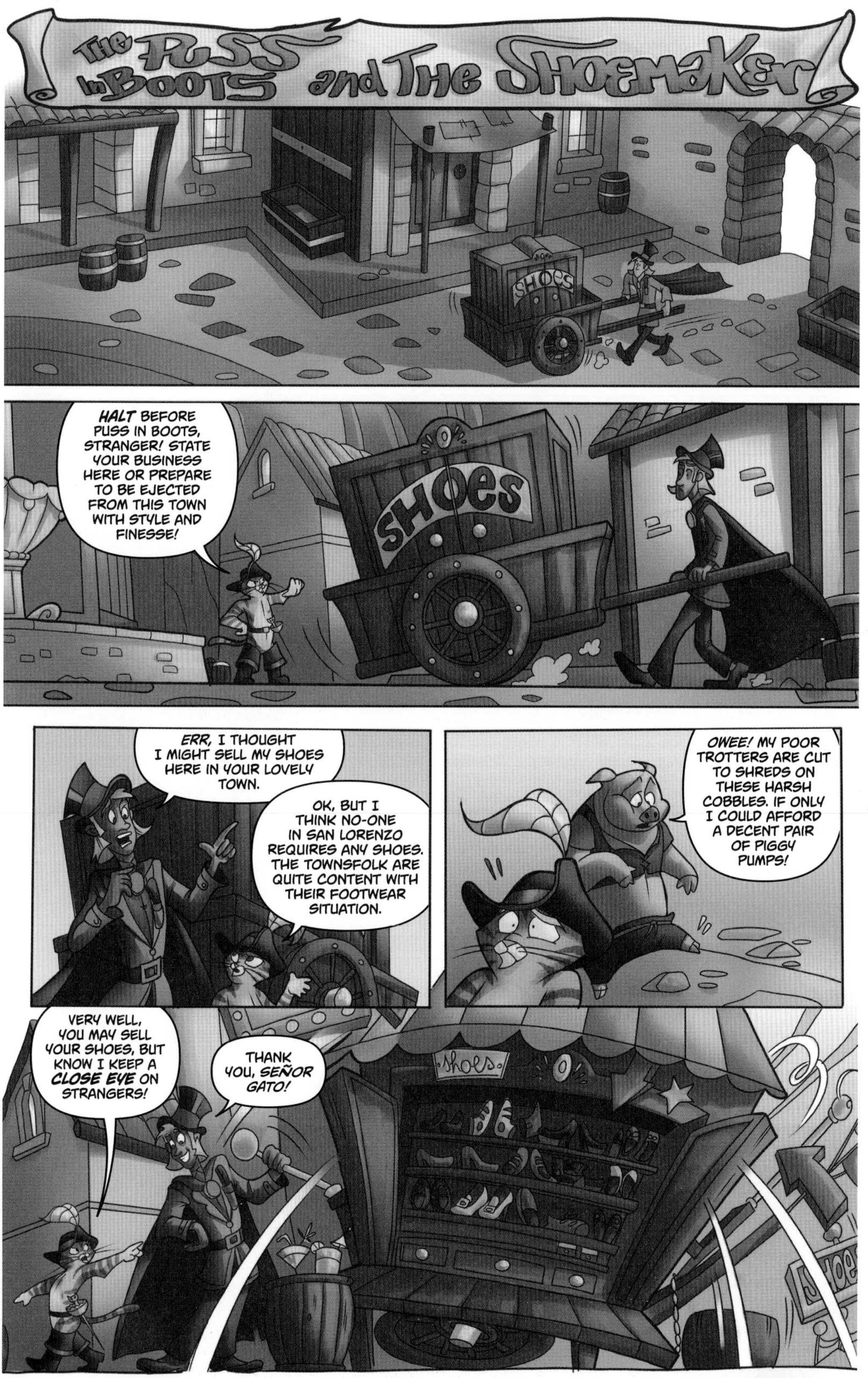
The Puss in Boots and The Shoemaker
SHOES
HALT BEFORE PUSS IN BOOTS, STRANGER! STATE YOUR BUSINESS HERE OR PREPARE TO BE EJECTED FROM THIS TOWN WITH STYLE AND FINESSE!
SHOES
ERR, I THOUGHT I MIGHT SELL MY SHOES HERE IN YOUR LOVELY TOWN.
OK, BUT I THINK NO-ONE IN SAN LORENZO REQUIRES ANY SHOES. THE TOWNSFOLK ARE QUITE CONTENT WITH THEIR FOOTWEAR SITUATION.
OWEE! MY POOR TROTTERS ARE CUT TO SHREDS ON THESE HARSH COBBLES. IF ONLY I COULD AFFORD A DECENT PAIR OF PIGGY PUMPS!
VERY WELL, YOU MAY SELL YOUR SHOES, BUT KNOW I KEEP A CLOSE EYE ON STRANGERS!
THANK YOU, SEÑOR GATO!
shoes
SHOES

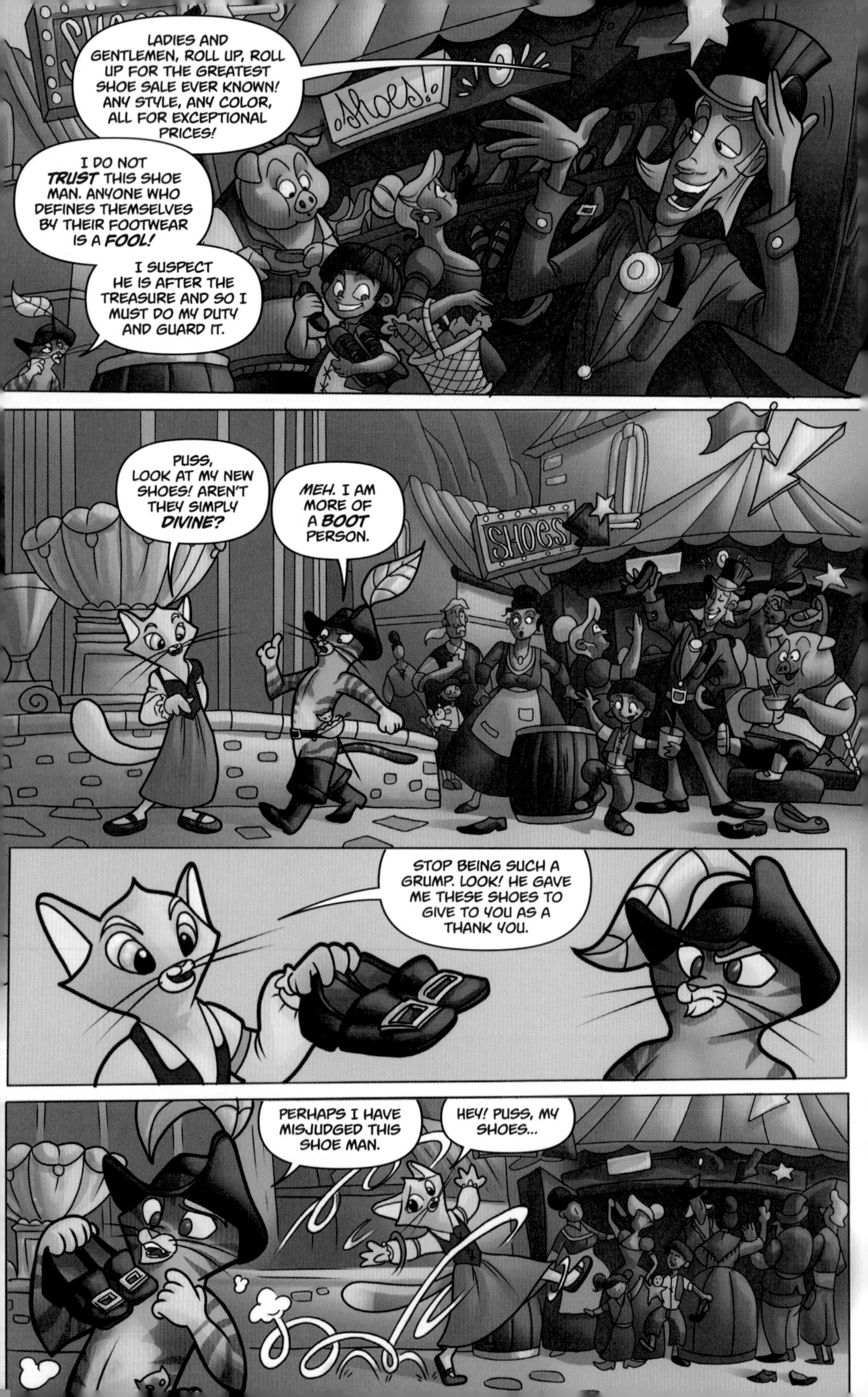

Shoes!
LADIES AND GENTLEMEN, ROLL UP, ROLL UP FOR THE GREATEST SHOE SALE EVER KNOWN! ANY STYLE, ANY COLOR, ALL FOR EXCEPTIONAL PRICES!
I DO NOT TRUST THIS SHOE MAN. ANYONE WHO DEFINES THEMSELVES BY THEIR FOOTWEAR IS A FOOL!
I SUSPECT HE IS AFTER THE TREASURE AND SO I MUST DO MY DUTY AND GUARD IT.
PUSS, LOOK AT MY NEW SHOES! AREN'T THEY SIMPLY DIVINE?
MEH. I AM MORE OF A BOOT PERSON.
SHOES
STOP BEING SUCH A GRUMP. LOOK! HE GAVE ME THESE SHOES TO GIVE TO YOU AS A THANK YOU.
PERHAPS I HAVE MISJUDGED THIS SHOE MAN.
HEY! PUSS, MY SHOES...

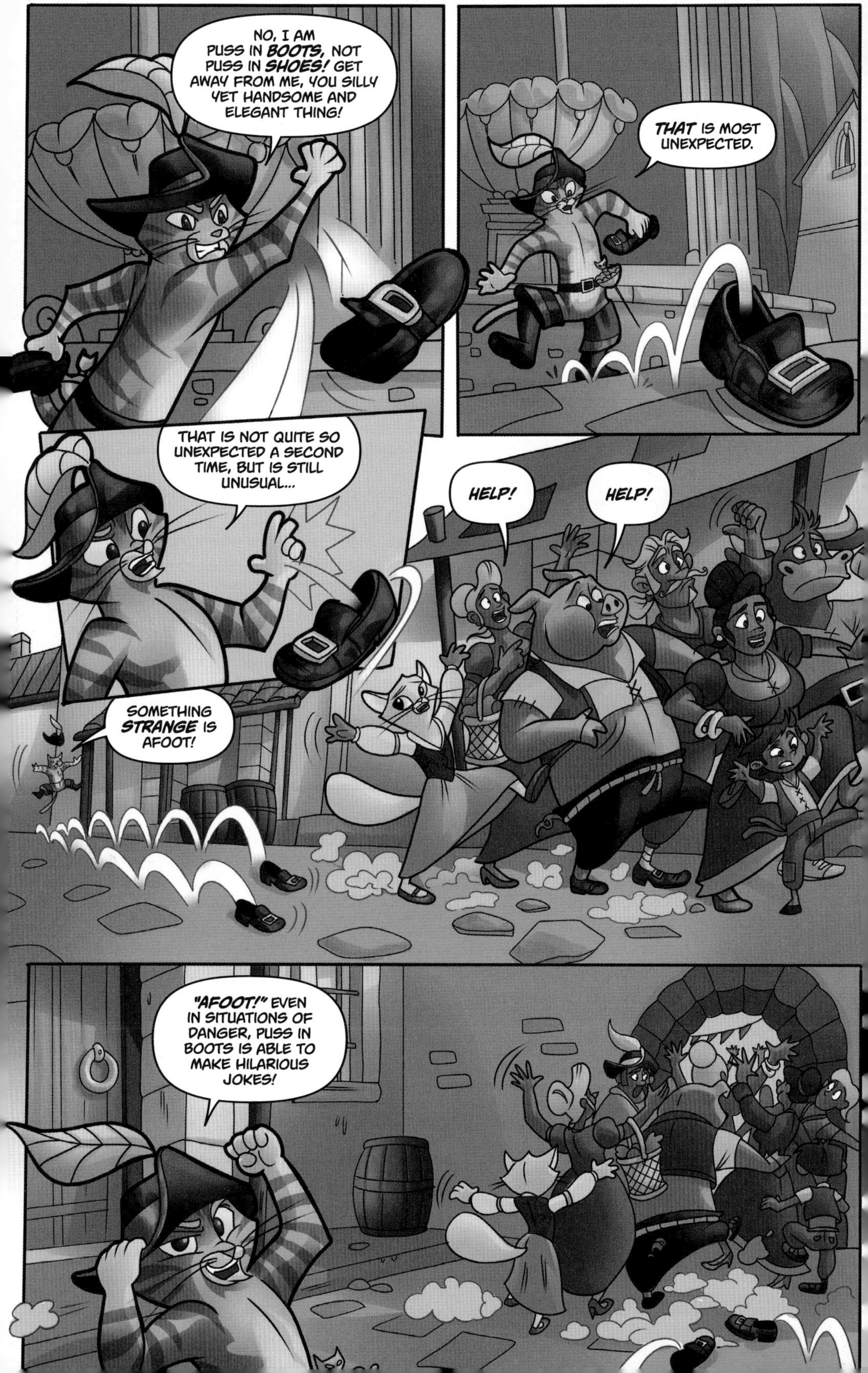
NO, I AM PUSS IN BOOTS, NOT PUSS IN SHOES! GET AWAY FROM ME, YOU SILLY YET HANDSOME AND ELEGANT THING!
THAT IS MOST UNEXPECTED.
THAT IS NOT QUITE SO UNEXPECTED A SECOND TIME, BUT IS STILL UNUSUAL...
HELP!
HELP!
SOMETHING STRANGE IS AFOOT!
"AFOOT!" EVEN IN SITUATIONS OF DANGER, PUSS IN BOOTS IS ABLE TO MAKE HILARIOUS JOKES!

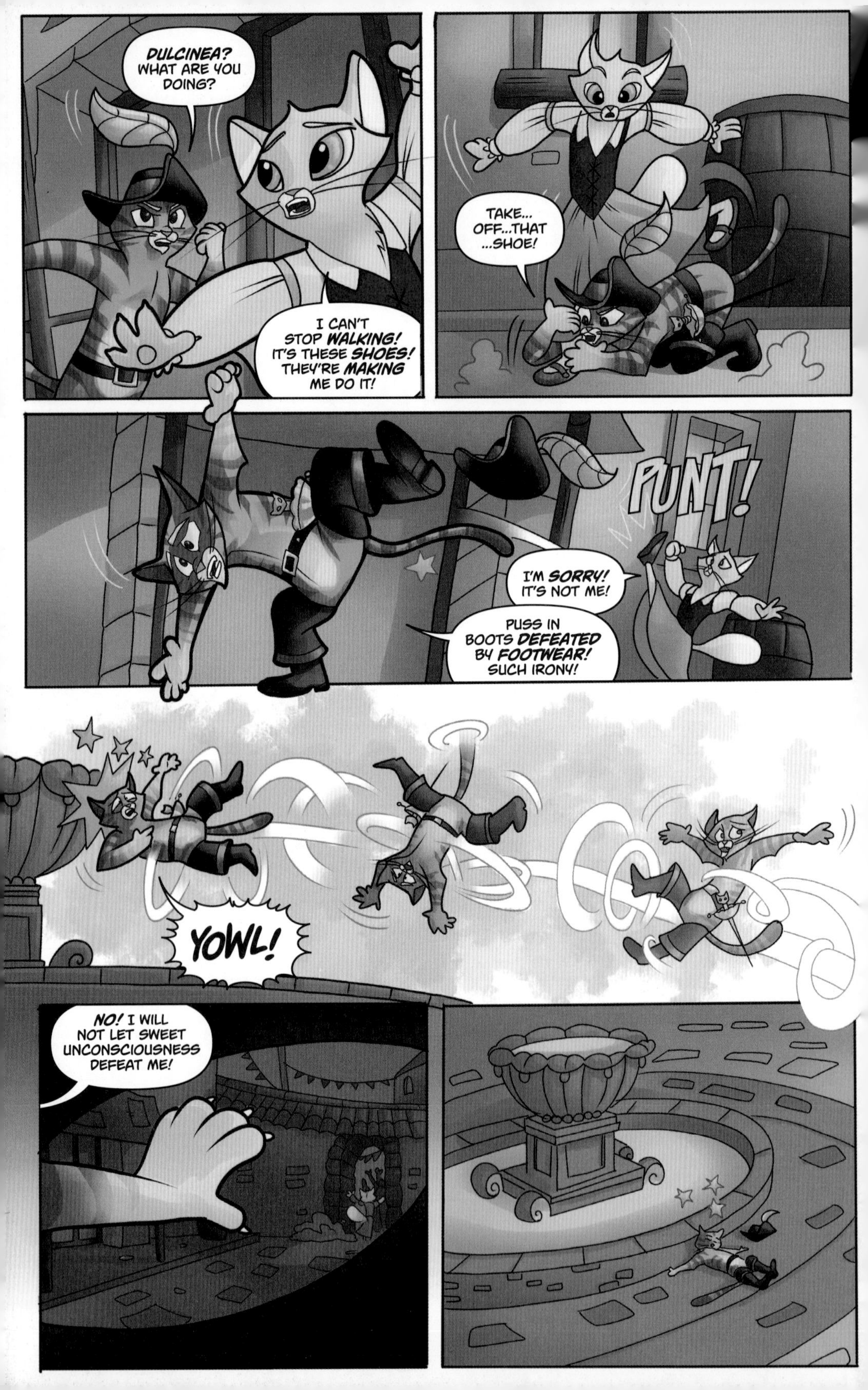
DULCINEA? WHAT ARE YOU DOING?
I CAN'T STOP WALKING! IT'S THESE SHOES! THEY'RE MAKING ME DO IT!
TAKE... OFF...THAT ...SHOE!
PUNT!
I'M SORRY! IT'S NOT ME!
PUSS IN BOOTS DEFEATED BY FOOTWEAR! SUCH IRONY!
YOWL!
NO! I WILL NOT LET SWEET UNCONSCIOUSNESS DEFEAT ME!

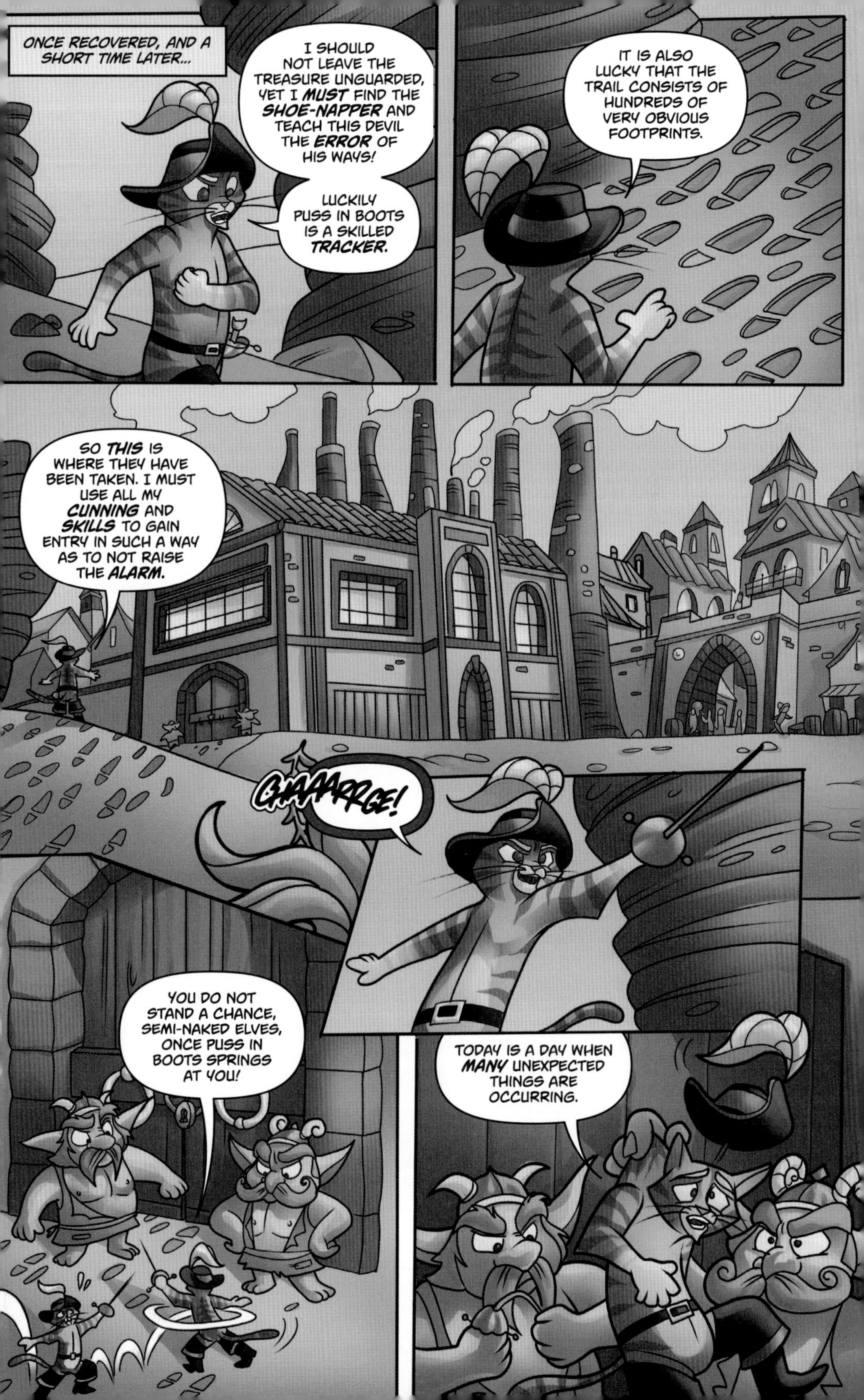
ONCE RECOVERED, AND A SHORT TIME LATER...
I SHOULD NOT LEAVE THE TREASURE UNGUARDED, YET I MUST FIND THE SHOE-NAPPER AND TEACH THIS DEVIL THE ERROR OF HIS WAYS!
LUCKILY PUSS IN BOOTS IS A SKILLED TRACKER.
IT IS ALSO LUCKY THAT THE TRAIL CONSISTS OF HUNDREDS OF VERY OBVIOUS FOOTPRINTS.
SO THIS IS WHERE THEY HAVE BEEN TAKEN. I MUST USE ALL MY CUNNING AND SKILLS TO GAIN ENTRY IN SUCH A WAY AS TO NOT RAISE THE ALARM.
CHAAAARRGE!
YOU DO NOT STAND A CHANCE, SEMI-NAKED ELVES, ONCE PUSS IN BOOTS SPRINGS AT YOU!
TODAY IS A DAY WHEN MANY UNEXPECTED THINGS ARE OCCURRING.

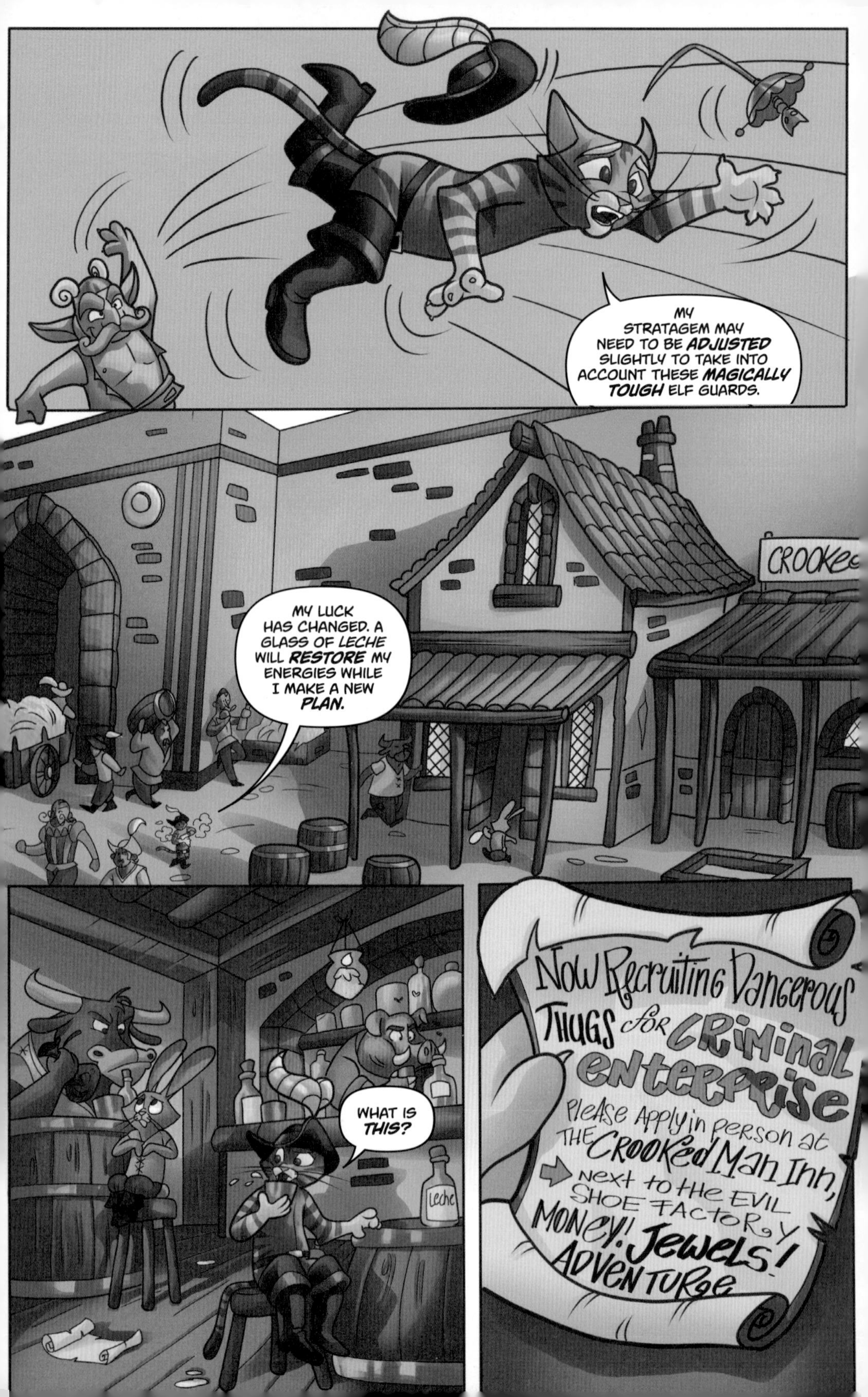
MY STRATAGEM MAY NEED TO BE ADJUSTED SLIGHTLY TO TAKE INTO ACCOUNT THESE MAGICALLY TOUGH ELF GUARDS.
CROOKE
MY LUCK HAS CHANGED. A GLASS OF LECHE WILL RESTORE MY ENERGIES WHILE I MAKE A NEW PLAN.
WHAT IS THIS?
Leche
Now Recruiting Dangerous Thugs for Criminal enterprise
Please Apply in person at the Crooked Man Inn,
next to the EVIL SHOE FACTORY
MONEY! JEWELS! ADVENTURE

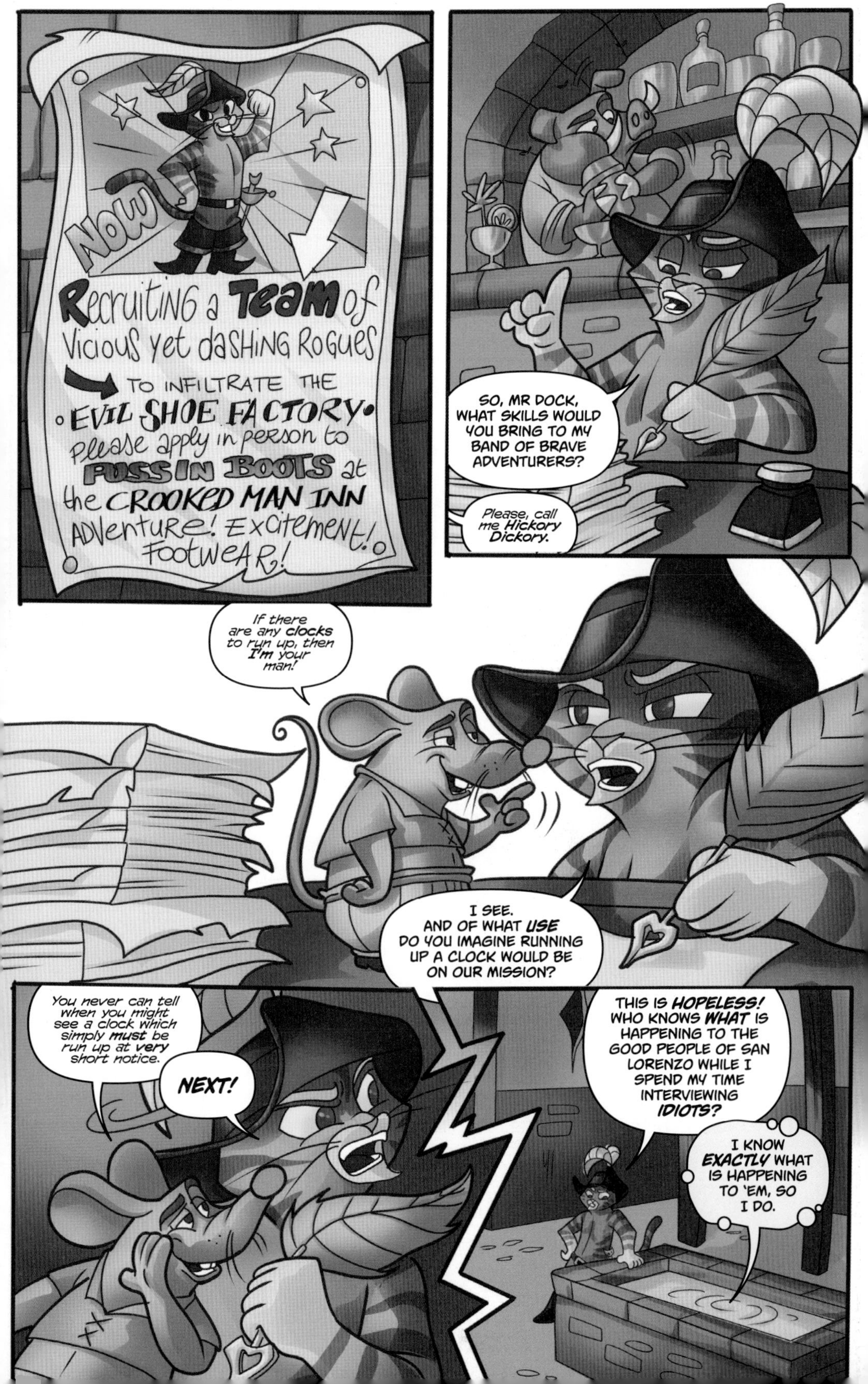

NOW
Recruiting a Team of Vicious yet dashing Rogues
TO INFILTRATE THE
EVIL SHOE FACTORY
Please apply in person to
PUSS IN BOOTS at
the CROOKED MAN INN
ADVENTURE! EXCITEMENT! FOOTWEAR!
SO, MR DOCK, WHAT SKILLS WOULD YOU BRING TO MY BAND OF BRAVE ADVENTURERS?
Please, call me Hickory Dickory.
If there are any clocks to run up, then I'm your man!
I SEE. AND OF WHAT USE DO YOU IMAGINE RUNNING UP A CLOCK WOULD BE ON OUR MISSION?
You never can tell when you might see a clock which simply must be run up at very short notice.
NEXT!
THIS IS HOPELESS! WHO KNOWS WHAT IS HAPPENING TO THE GOOD PEOPLE OF SAN LORENZO WHILE I SPEND MY TIME INTERVIEWING IDIOTS?
I KNOW EXACTLY WHAT IS HAPPENING TO 'EM, SO I DO.

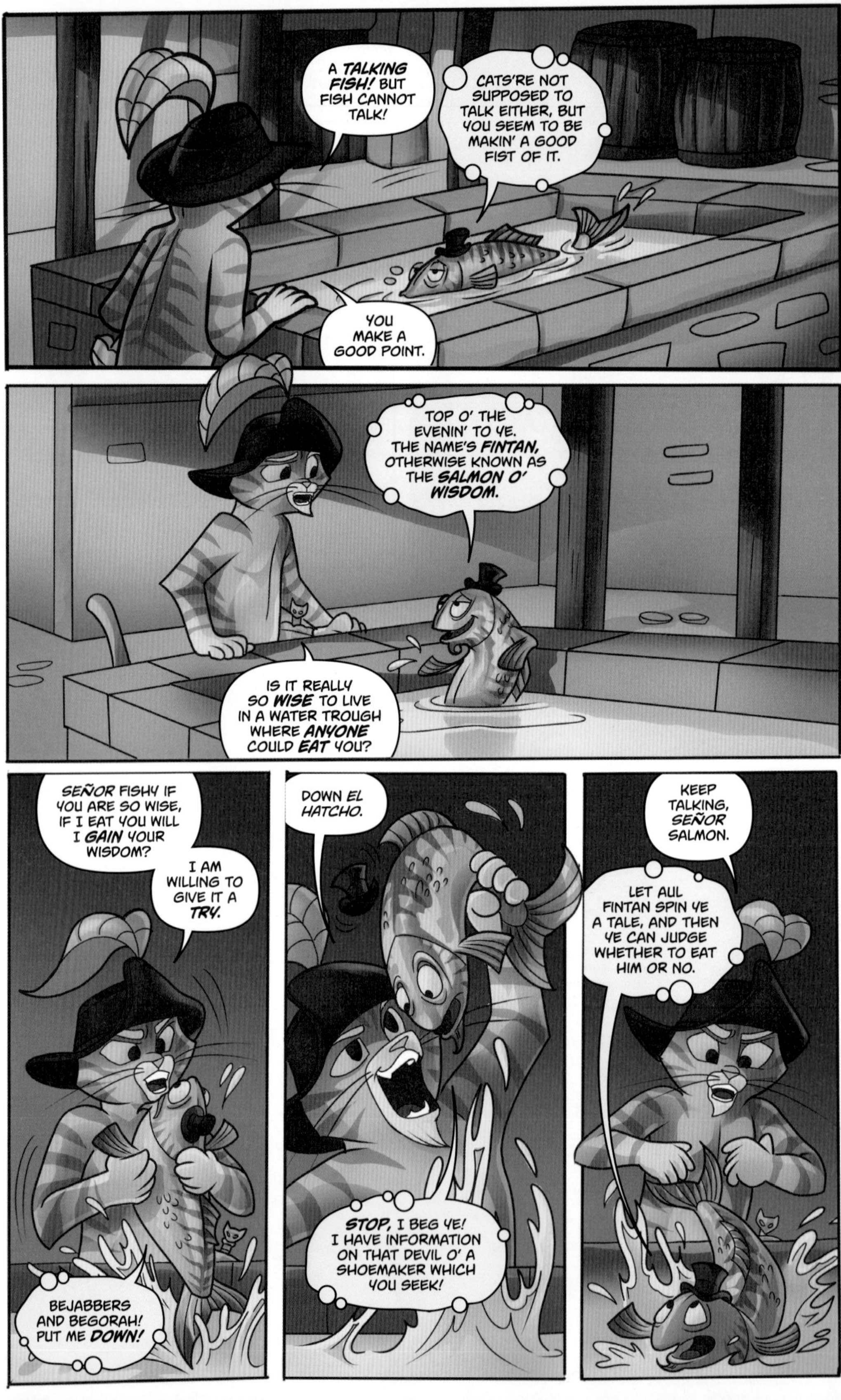
A TALKING FISH! BUT FISH CANNOT TALK!
CATS'RE NOT SUPPOSED TO TALK EITHER, BUT YOU SEEM TO BE MAKIN' A GOOD FIST OF IT.
YOU MAKE A GOOD POINT.
TOP O' THE EVENIN' TO YE. THE NAME'S FINTAN, OTHERWISE KNOWN AS THE SALMON O' WISDOM.
IS IT REALLY SO WISE TO LIVE IN A WATER TROUGH WHERE ANYONE COULD EAT YOU?
SEÑOR FISHY IF YOU ARE SO WISE, IF I EAT YOU WILL I GAIN YOUR WISDOM?
I AM WILLING TO GIVE IT A TRY.
BEJABBERS AND BEGORAH! PUT ME DOWN!
DOWN EL HATCHO.
STOP, I BEG YE! I HAVE INFORMATION ON THAT DEVIL O' A SHOEMAKER WHICH YOU SEEK!
KEEP TALKING, SEÑOR SALMON.
LET AUL FINTAN SPIN YE A TALE, AND THEN YE CAN JUDGE WHETHER TO EAT HIM OR NO.

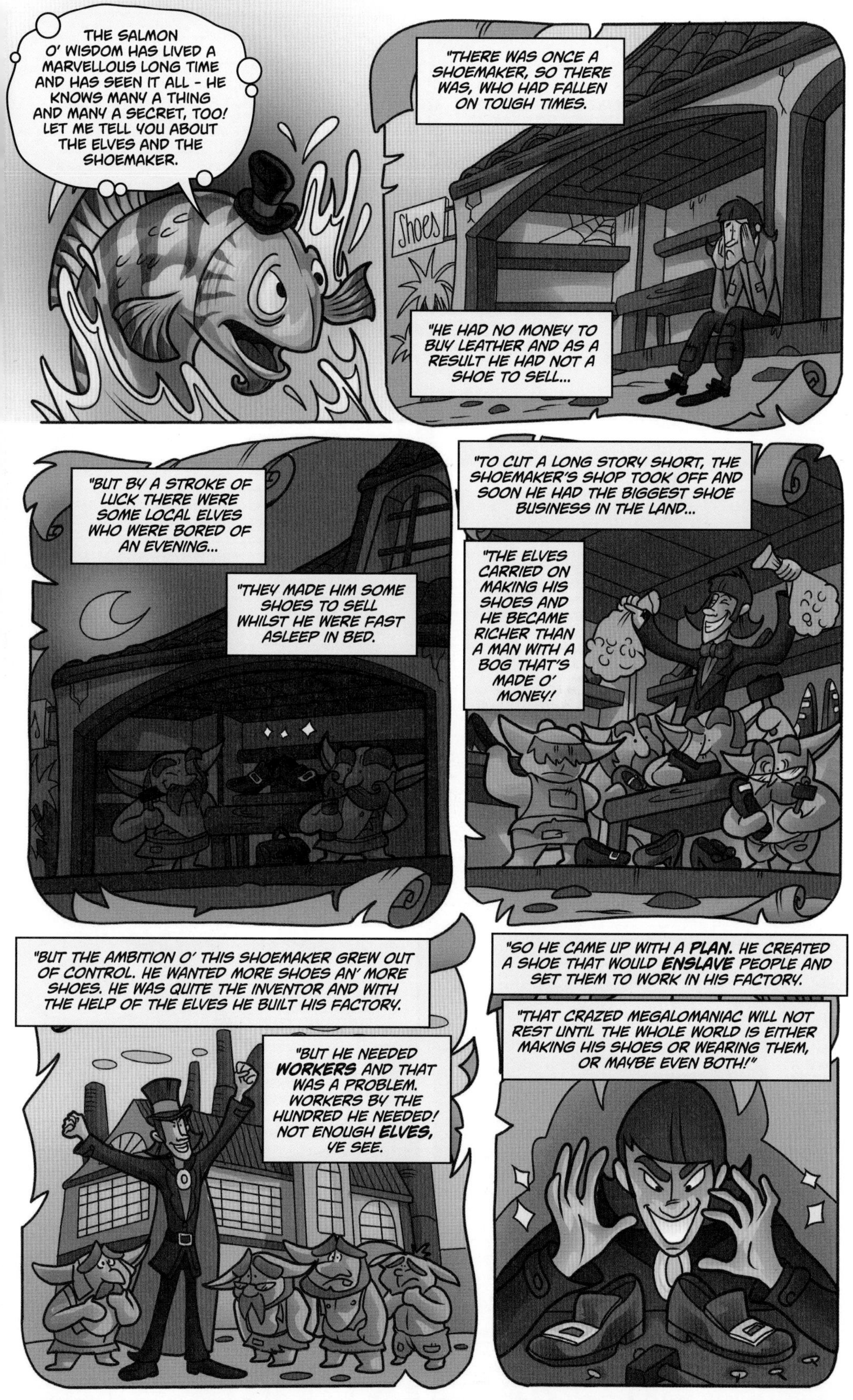
THE SALMON O' WISDOM HAS LIVED A MARVELLOUS LONG TIME AND HAS SEEN IT ALL - HE KNOWS MANY A THING AND MANY A SECRET, TOO! LET ME TELL YOU ABOUT THE ELVES AND THE SHOEMAKER.
"THERE WAS ONCE A SHOEMAKER, SO THERE WAS, WHO HAD FALLEN ON TOUGH TIMES.
Shoes
"HE HAD NO MONEY TO BUY LEATHER AND AS A RESULT HE HAD NOT A SHOE TO SELL...
"BUT BY A STROKE OF LUCK THERE WERE SOME LOCAL ELVES WHO WERE BORED OF AN EVENING...
"THEY MADE HIM SOME SHOES TO SELL WHILST HE WERE FAST ASLEEP IN BED.
"TO CUT A LONG STORY SHORT, THE SHOEMAKER'S SHOP TOOK OFF AND SOON HE HAD THE BIGGEST SHOE BUSINESS IN THE LAND...
"THE ELVES CARRIED ON MAKING HIS SHOES AND HE BECAME RICHER THAN A MAN WITH A BOG THAT'S MADE O' MONEY!
"BUT THE AMBITION O' THIS SHOEMAKER GREW OUT OF CONTROL. HE WANTED MORE SHOES AN' MORE SHOES. HE WAS QUITE THE INVENTOR AND WITH THE HELP OF THE ELVES HE BUILT HIS FACTORY.
"BUT HE NEEDED **WORKERS** AND THAT WAS A PROBLEM. WORKERS BY THE HUNDRED HE NEEDED! NOT ENOUGH **ELVES,** YE SEE.
"SO HE CAME UP WITH A **PLAN.** HE CREATED A SHOE THAT WOULD **ENSLAVE** PEOPLE AND SET THEM TO WORK IN HIS FACTORY.
"THAT CRAZED MEGALOMANIAC WILL NOT REST UNTIL THE WHOLE WORLD IS EITHER MAKING HIS SHOES OR WEARING THEM, OR MAYBE EVEN BOTH!"

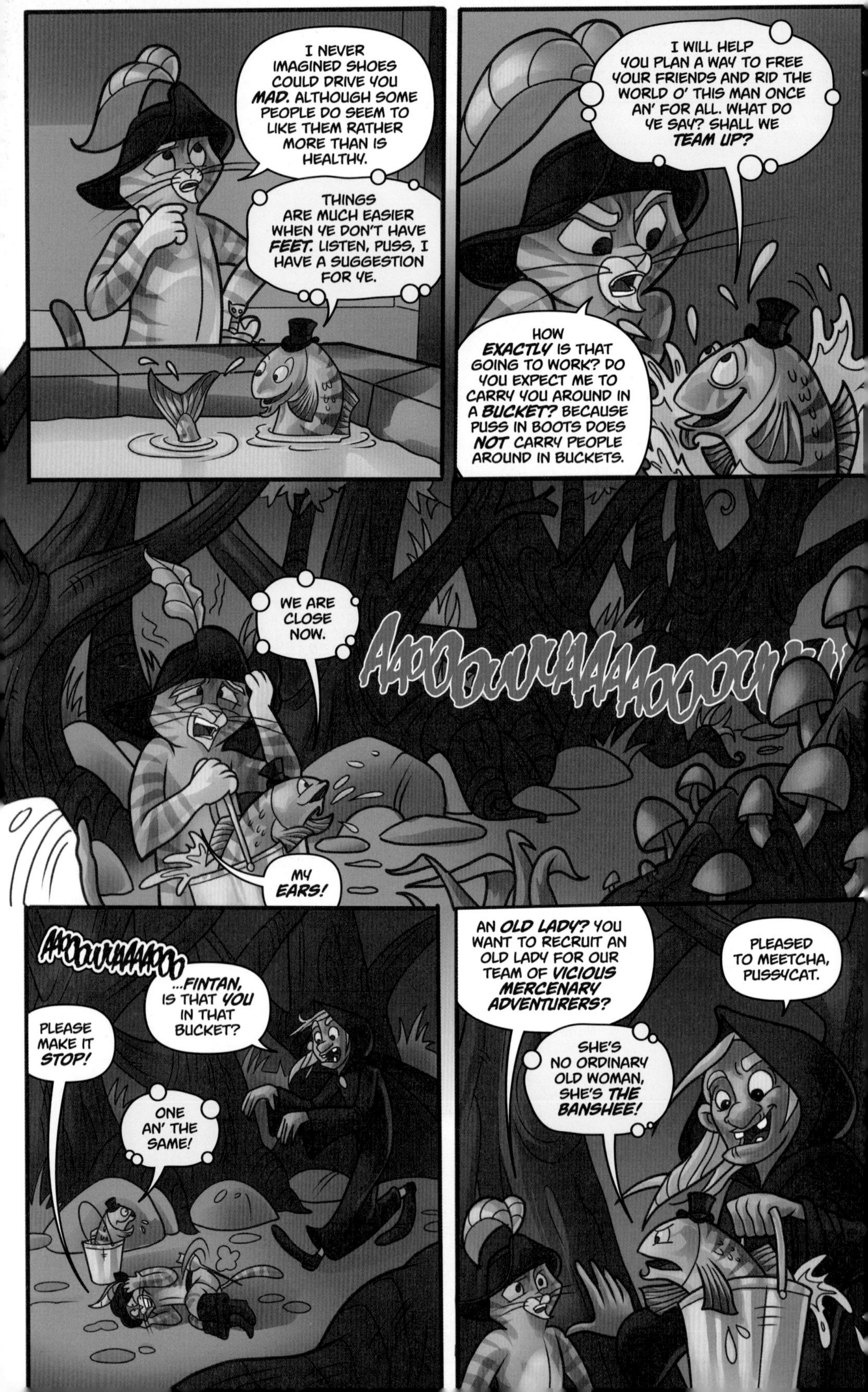
I NEVER IMAGINED SHOES COULD DRIVE YOU **MAD.** ALTHOUGH SOME PEOPLE DO SEEM TO LIKE THEM RATHER MORE THAN IS HEALTHY.
THINGS ARE MUCH EASIER WHEN YE DON'T HAVE **FEET.** LISTEN, PUSS, I HAVE A SUGGESTION FOR YE.
I WILL HELP YOU PLAN A WAY TO FREE YOUR FRIENDS AND RID THE WORLD O' THIS MAN ONCE AN' FOR ALL. WHAT DO YE SAY? SHALL WE **TEAM UP?**
HOW **EXACTLY** IS THAT GOING TO WORK? DO YOU EXPECT ME TO CARRY YOU AROUND IN A **BUCKET?** BECAUSE PUSS IN BOOTS DOES **NOT** CARRY PEOPLE AROUND IN BUCKETS.
WE ARE CLOSE NOW.
MY **EARS!**
...**FINTAN,** IS THAT **YOU** IN THAT BUCKET?
PLEASE MAKE IT **STOP!**
ONE AN' THE SAME!
AN **OLD LADY?** YOU WANT TO RECRUIT AN OLD LADY FOR OUR TEAM OF **VICIOUS MERCENARY ADVENTURERS?**
SHE'S NO ORDINARY OLD WOMAN, SHE'S **THE BANSHEE!**
PLEASED TO MEETCHA, PUSSYCAT.

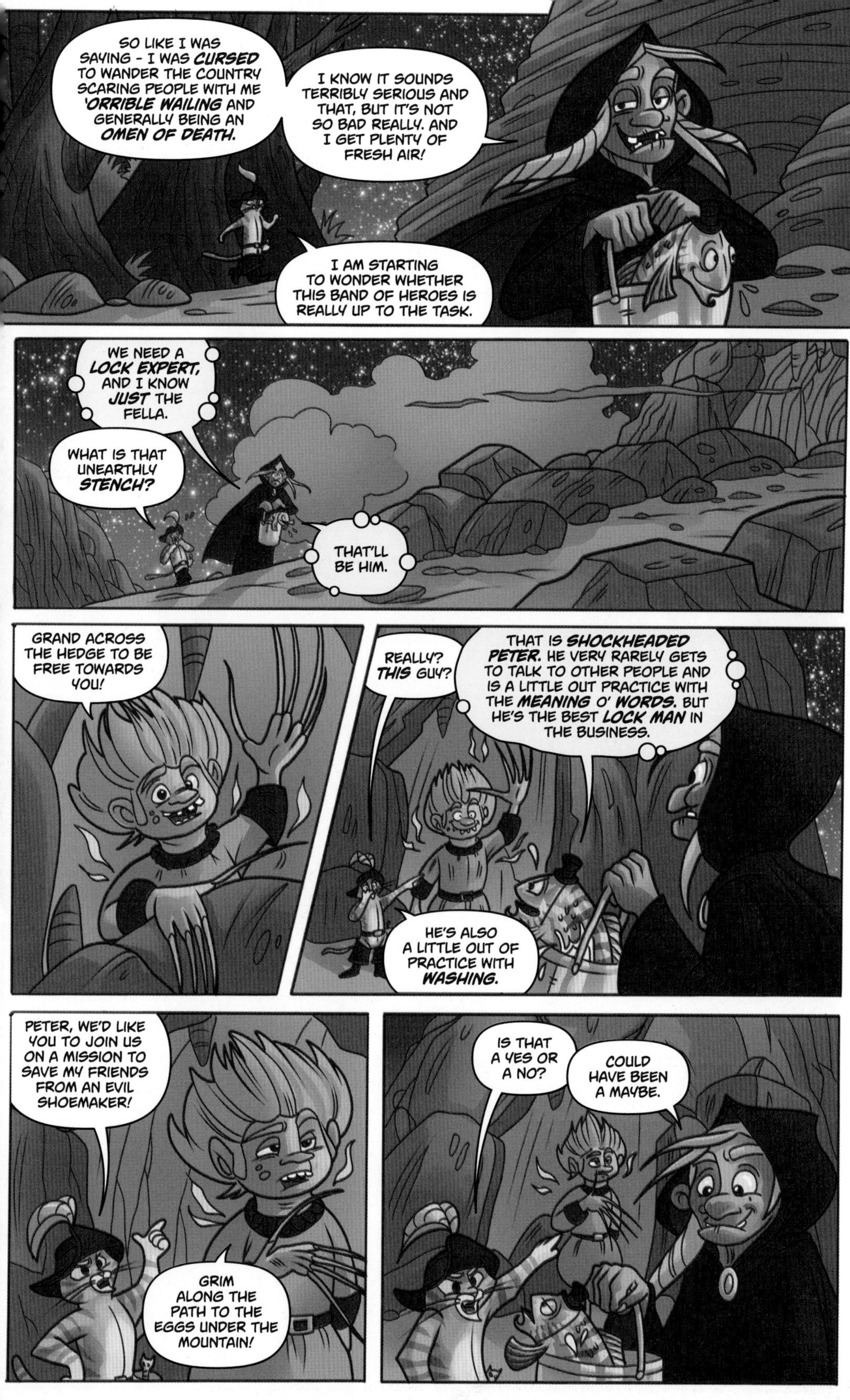
SO LIKE I WAS SAYING - I WAS CURSED TO WANDER THE COUNTRY SCARING PEOPLE WITH ME 'ORRIBLE WAILING AND GENERALLY BEING AN OMEN OF DEATH.
I KNOW IT SOUNDS TERRIBLY SERIOUS AND THAT, BUT IT'S NOT SO BAD REALLY. AND I GET PLENTY OF FRESH AIR!
I AM STARTING TO WONDER WHETHER THIS BAND OF HEROES IS REALLY UP TO THE TASK.
WE NEED A LOCK EXPERT, AND I KNOW JUST THE FELLA.
WHAT IS THAT UNEARTHLY STENCH?
THAT'LL BE HIM.
GRAND ACROSS THE HEDGE TO BE FREE TOWARDS YOU!
REALLY? THIS GUY?
THAT IS SHOCKHEADED PETER. HE VERY RARELY GETS TO TALK TO OTHER PEOPLE AND IS A LITTLE OUT PRACTICE WITH THE MEANING O' WORDS. BUT HE'S THE BEST LOCK MAN IN THE BUSINESS.
HE'S ALSO A LITTLE OUT OF PRACTICE WITH WASHING.
PETER, WE'D LIKE YOU TO JOIN US ON A MISSION TO SAVE MY FRIENDS FROM AN EVIL SHOEMAKER!
GRIM ALONG THE PATH TO THE EGGS UNDER THE MOUNTAIN!
IS THAT A YES OR A NO?
COULD HAVE BEEN A MAYBE.

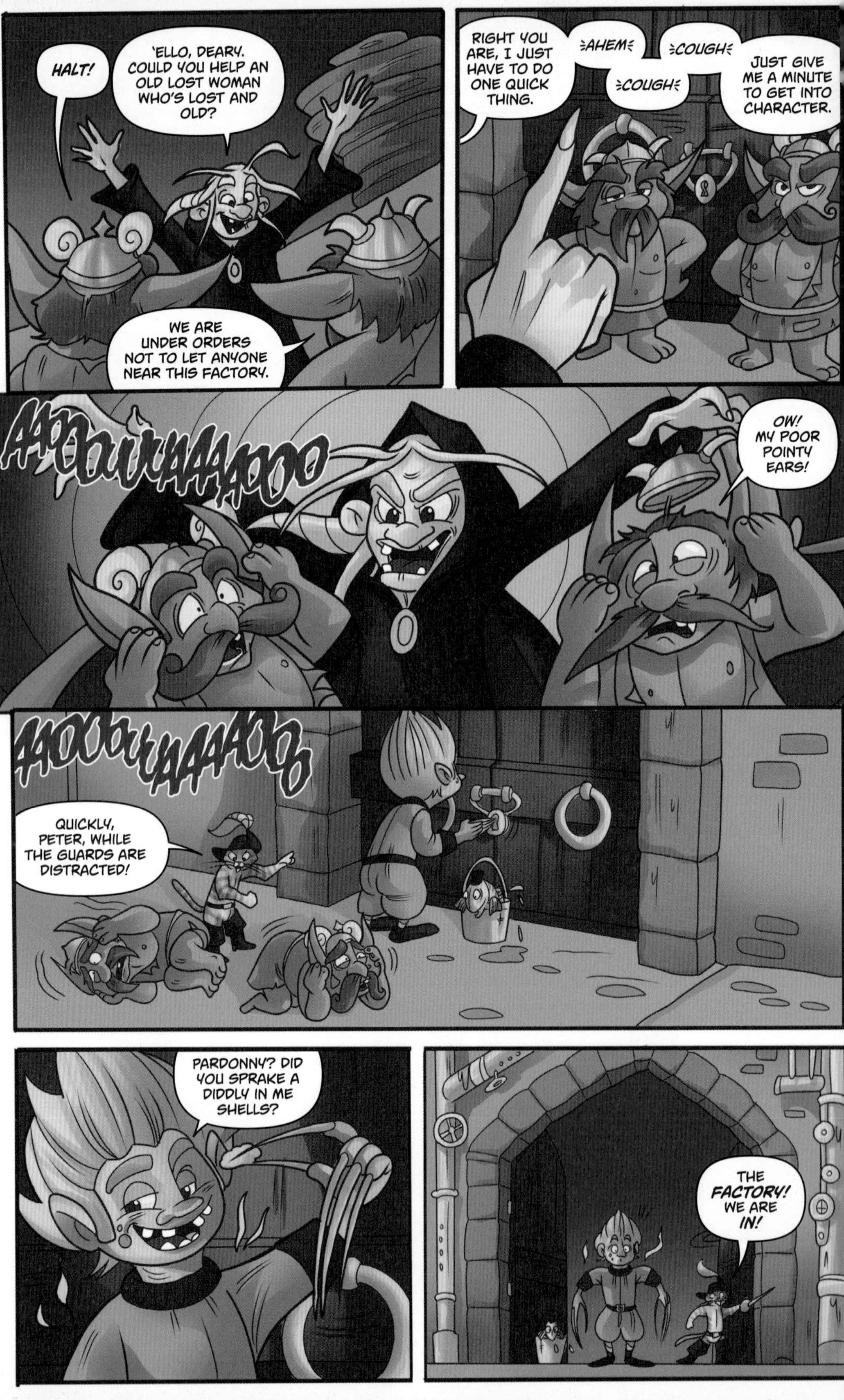
HALT!
'ELLO, DEARY. COULD YOU HELP AN OLD LOST WOMAN WHO'S LOST AND OLD?
WE ARE UNDER ORDERS NOT TO LET ANYONE NEAR THIS FACTORY.
RIGHT YOU ARE, I JUST HAVE TO DO ONE QUICK THING.
AHEM
COUGH
COUGH
JUST GIVE ME A MINUTE TO GET INTO CHARACTER.
OW! MY POOR POINTY EARS!
QUICKLY, PETER, WHILE THE GUARDS ARE DISTRACTED!
PARDONNY? DID YOU SPRAKE A DIDDLY IN ME SHELLS?
THE *FACTORY!* WE ARE *IN!*

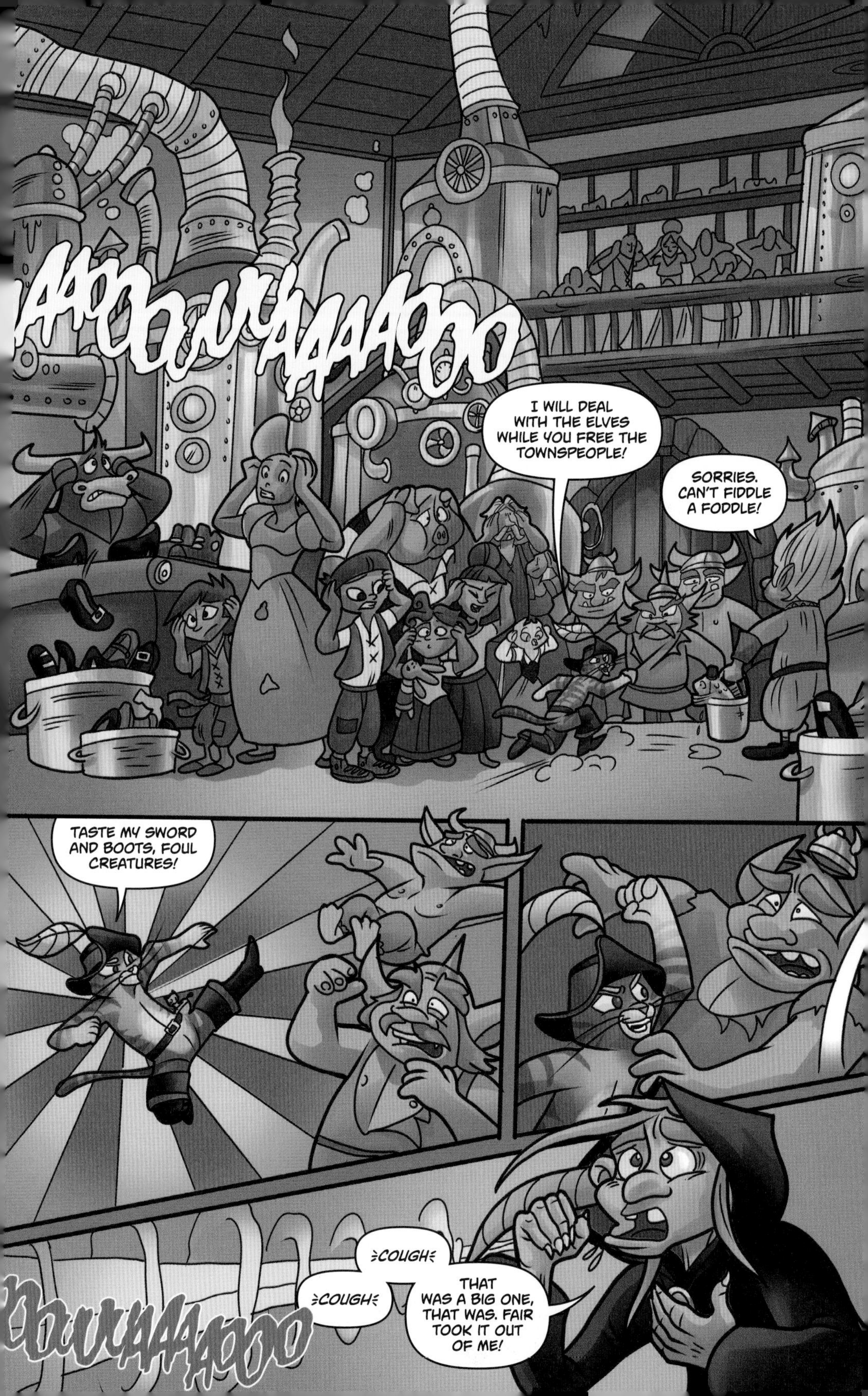
AAOOUUUAAAAOOO
I WILL DEAL WITH THE ELVES WHILE YOU FREE THE TOWNSPEOPLE!
SORRIES. CAN'T FIDDLE A FODDLE!
TASTE MY SWORD AND BOOTS, FOUL CREATURES!
OOUUAAAOOO
COUGH
COUGH
THAT WAS A BIG ONE, THAT WAS. FAIR TOOK IT OUT OF ME!

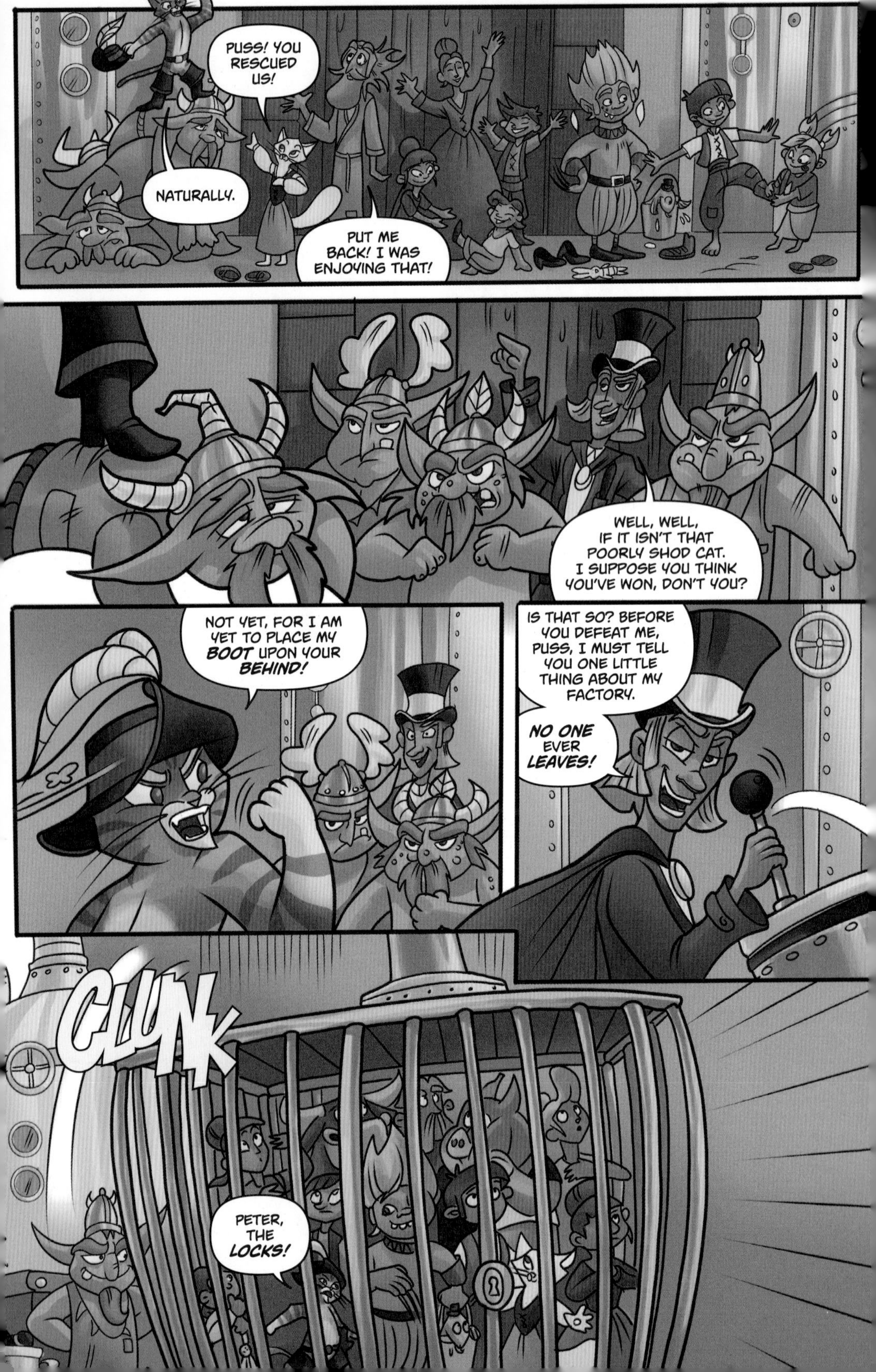
PUSS! YOU RESCUED US!
NATURALLY.
PUT ME BACK! I WAS ENJOYING THAT!
WELL, WELL, IF IT ISN'T THAT POORLY SHOD CAT. I SUPPOSE YOU THINK YOU'VE WON, DON'T YOU?
NOT YET, FOR I AM YET TO PLACE MY BOOT UPON YOUR BEHIND!
IS THAT SO? BEFORE YOU DEFEAT ME, PUSS, I MUST TELL YOU ONE LITTLE THING ABOUT MY FACTORY.
NO ONE EVER LEAVES!
CLUNK
PETER, THE LOCKS!

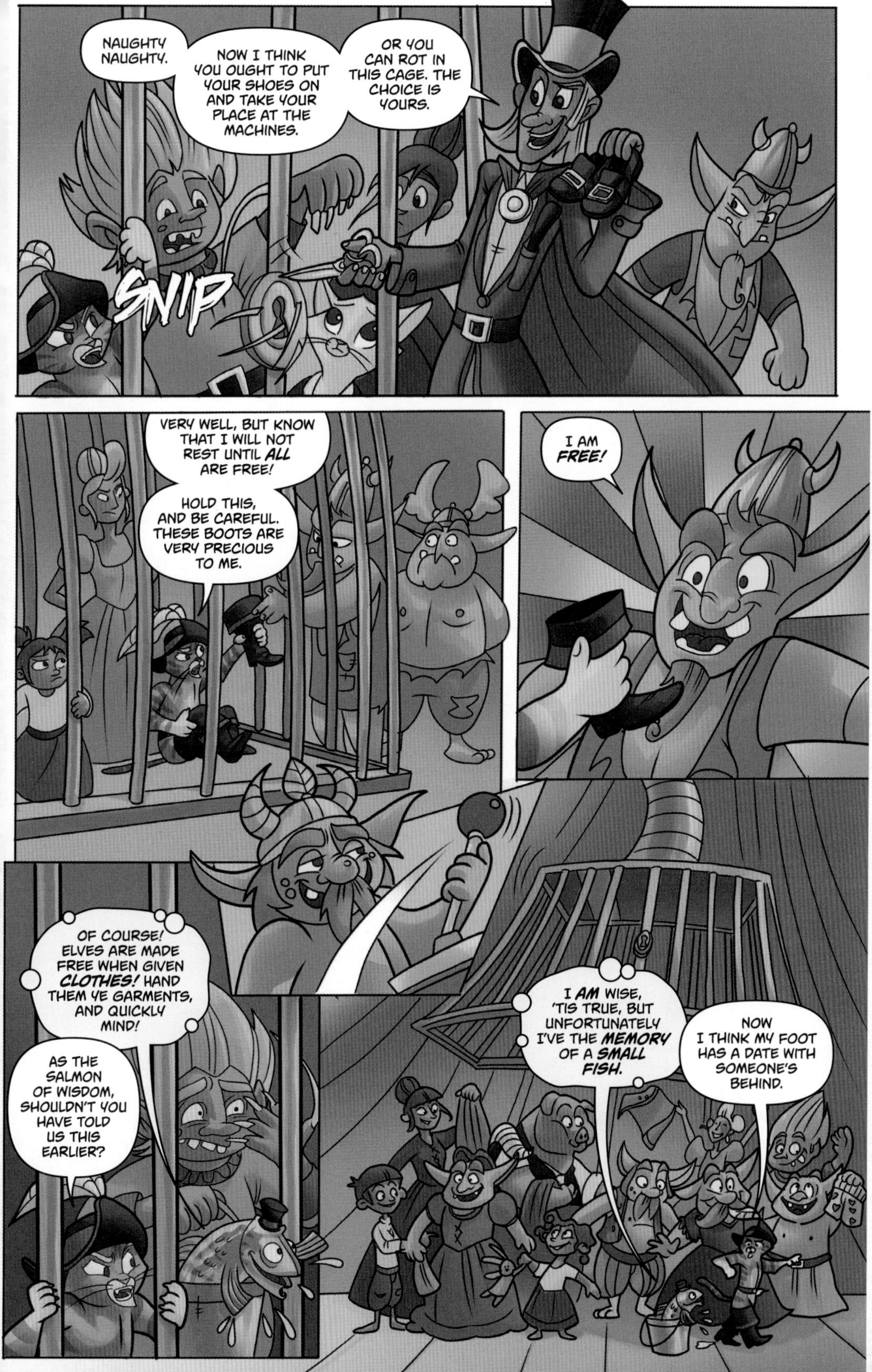
NAUGHTY NAUGHTY.
NOW I THINK YOU OUGHT TO PUT YOUR SHOES ON AND TAKE YOUR PLACE AT THE MACHINES.
OR YOU CAN ROT IN THIS CAGE. THE CHOICE IS YOURS.
SNIP
VERY WELL, BUT KNOW THAT I WILL NOT REST UNTIL ALL ARE FREE!
HOLD THIS, AND BE CAREFUL. THESE BOOTS ARE VERY PRECIOUS TO ME.
I AM FREE!
OF COURSE! ELVES ARE MADE FREE WHEN GIVEN CLOTHES! HAND THEM YE GARMENTS, AND QUICKLY MIND!
AS THE SALMON OF WISDOM, SHOULDN'T YOU HAVE TOLD US THIS EARLIER?
I AM WISE, 'TIS TRUE, BUT UNFORTUNATELY I'VE THE MEMORY OF A SMALL FISH.
NOW I THINK MY FOOT HAS A DATE WITH SOMEONE'S BEHIND.

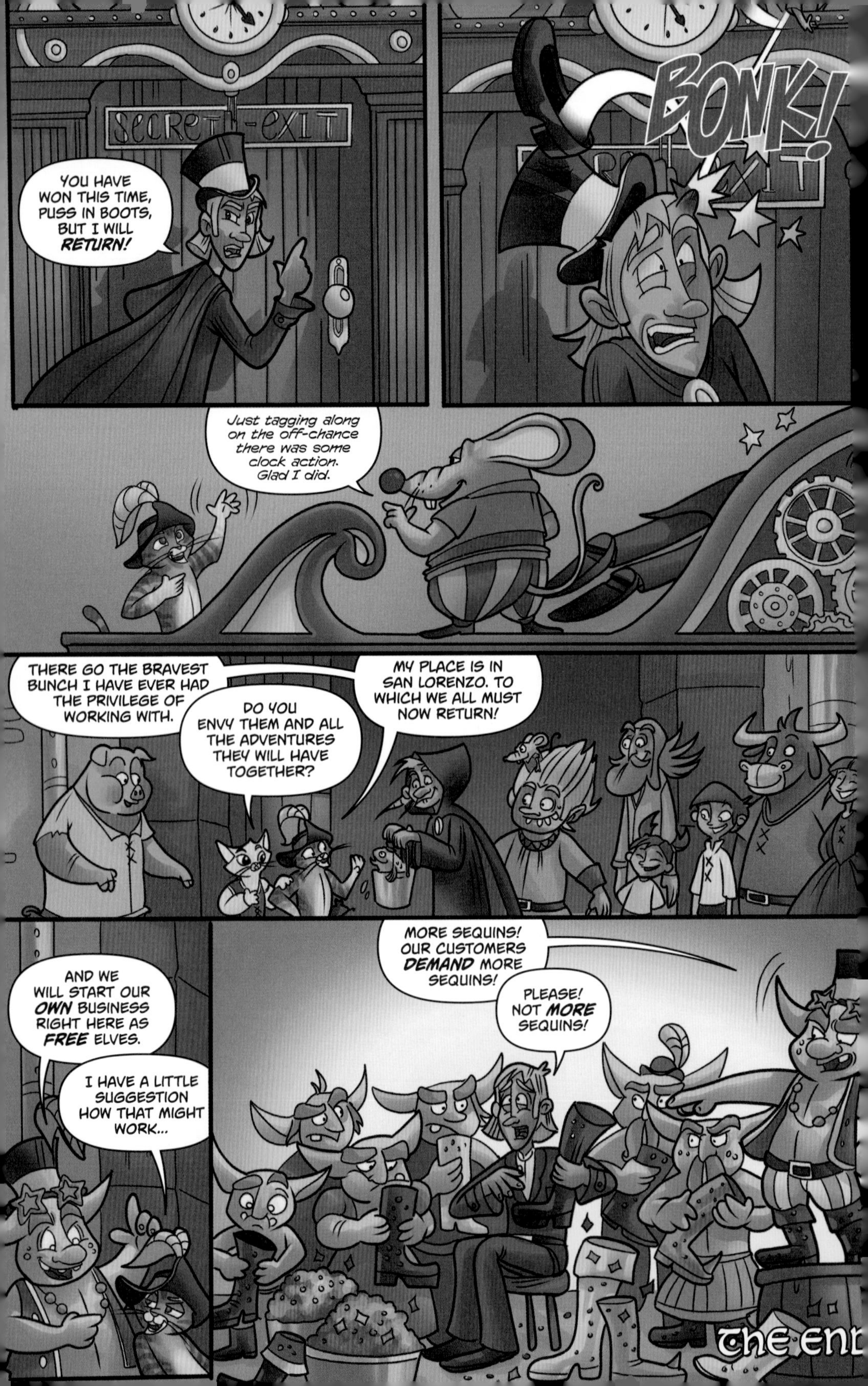
SECRET-EXIT
YOU HAVE WON THIS TIME, PUSS IN BOOTS, BUT I WILL *RETURN!*
BONK!
Just tagging along on the off-chance there was some clock action. Glad I did.
THERE GO THE BRAVEST BUNCH I HAVE EVER HAD THE PRIVILEGE OF WORKING WITH.
DO YOU ENVY THEM AND ALL THE ADVENTURES THEY WILL HAVE TOGETHER?
MY PLACE IS IN SAN LORENZO. TO WHICH WE ALL MUST NOW RETURN!
AND WE WILL START OUR *OWN* BUSINESS RIGHT HERE AS *FREE* ELVES.
I HAVE A LITTLE SUGGESTION HOW THAT MIGHT WORK...
MORE SEQUINS! OUR CUSTOMERS *DEMAND* MORE SEQUINS!
PLEASE! NOT *MORE* SEQUINS!
THE END

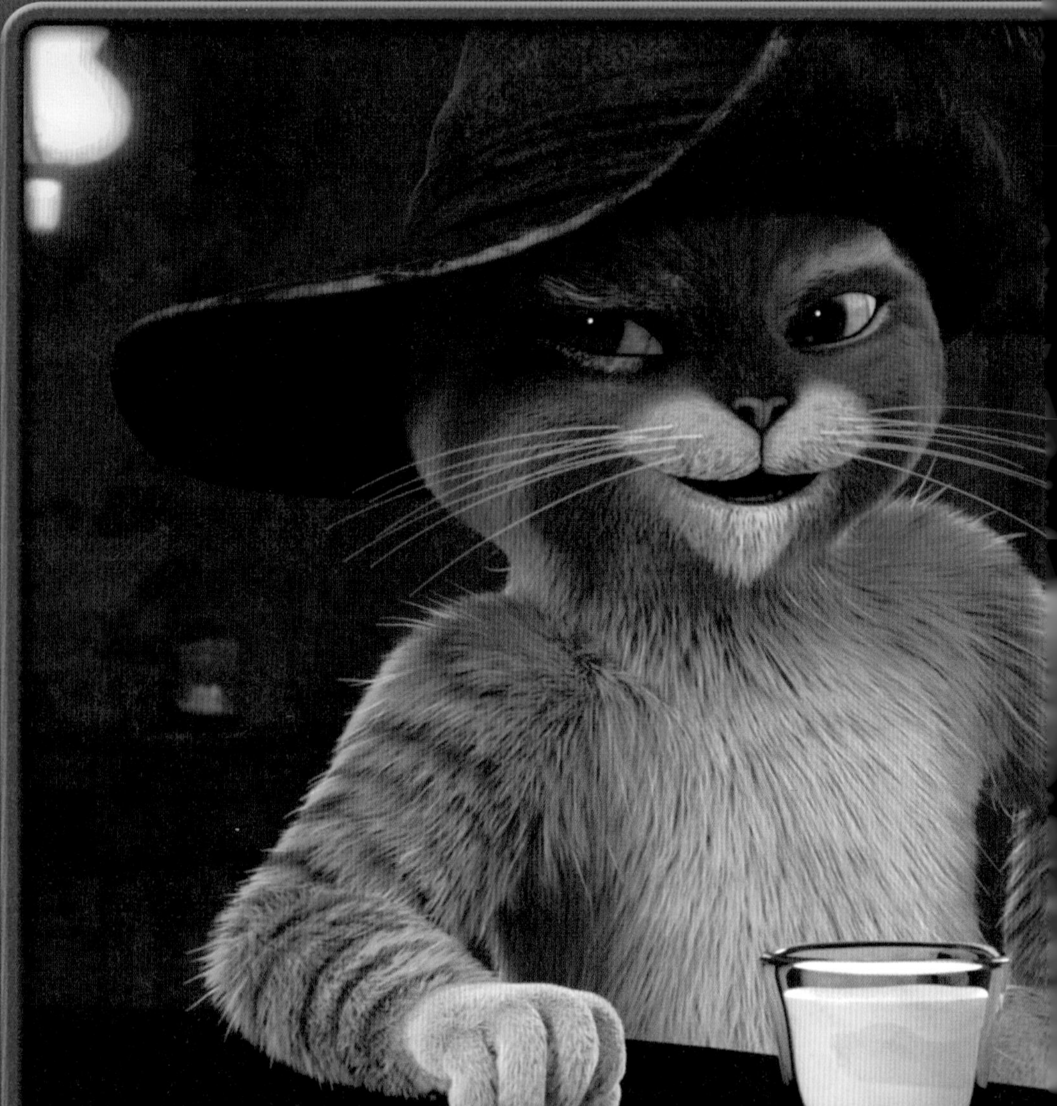

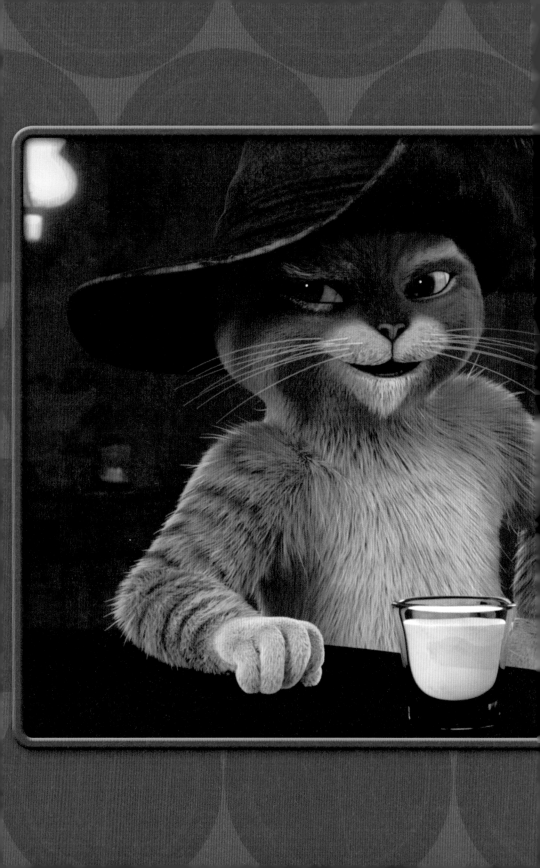

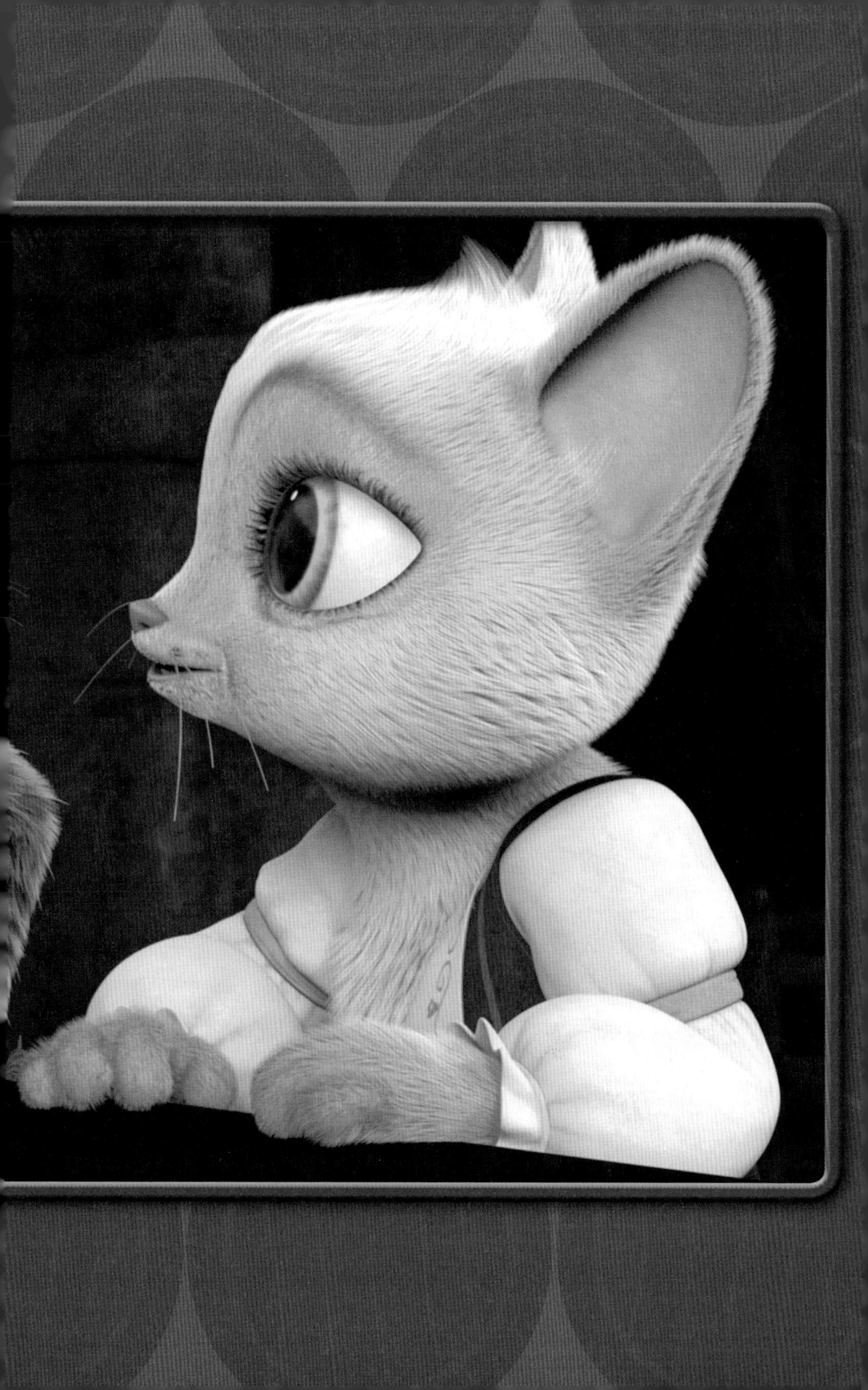

AS THE SAYING GOES

SCRIPT BY MAX DAVISON • PENCILS AND INKS BY DAVE ALVAREZ • COLORS BY PHIL ELLIOT • LETTERING BY JIM CAMPBELL

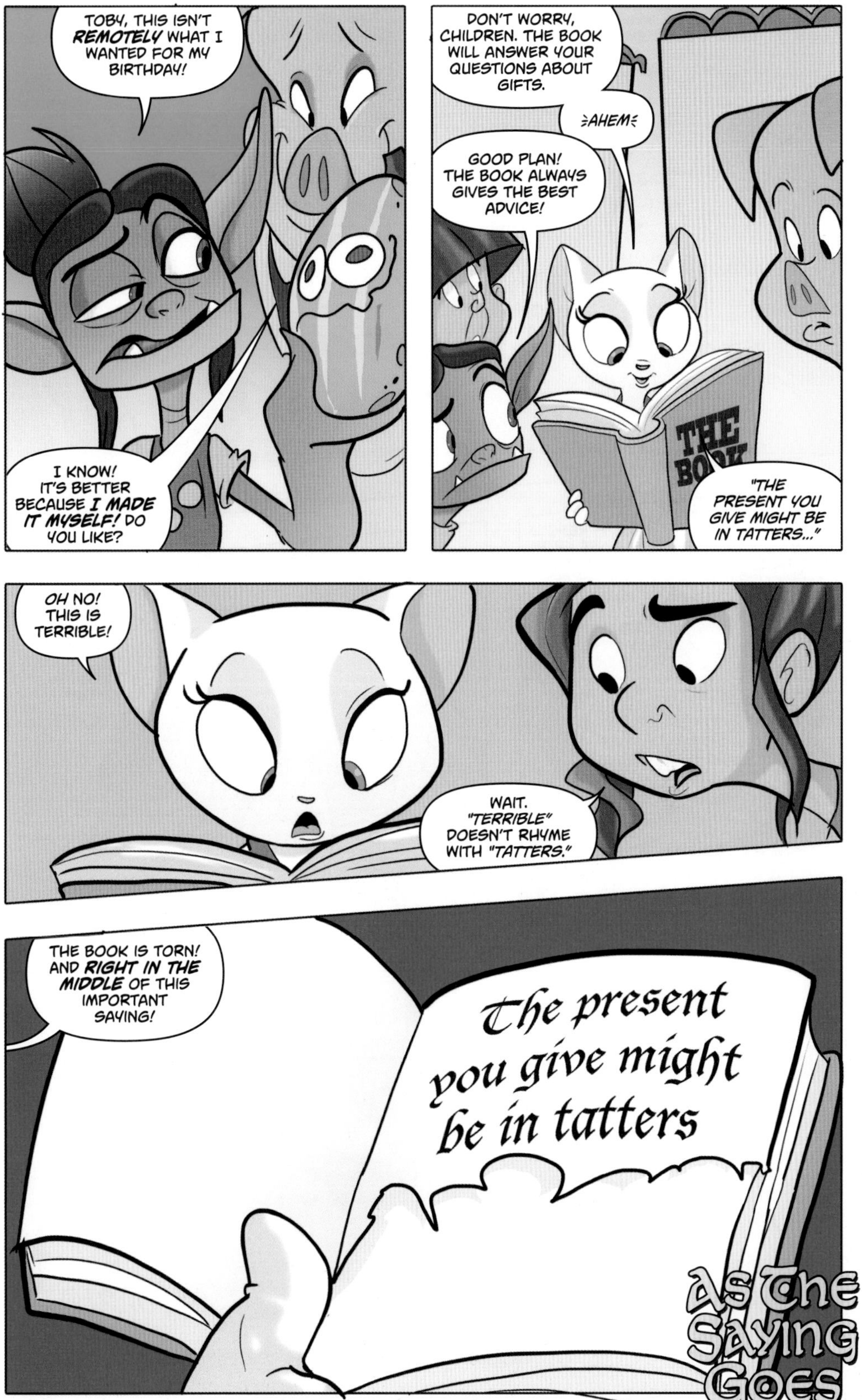
TOBY, THIS ISN'T REMOTELY WHAT I WANTED FOR MY BIRTHDAY!
I KNOW! IT'S BETTER BECAUSE I MADE IT MYSELF! DO YOU LIKE?
DON'T WORRY, CHILDREN. THE BOOK WILL ANSWER YOUR QUESTIONS ABOUT GIFTS.
AHEM
GOOD PLAN! THE BOOK ALWAYS GIVES THE BEST ADVICE!
THE BOOK
"THE PRESENT YOU GIVE MIGHT BE IN TATTERS..."
OH NO! THIS IS TERRIBLE!
WAIT. "TERRIBLE" DOESN'T RHYME WITH "TATTERS."
THE BOOK IS TORN! AND RIGHT IN THE MIDDLE OF THIS IMPORTANT SAYING!
The present you give might be in tatters
As The Saying Goes

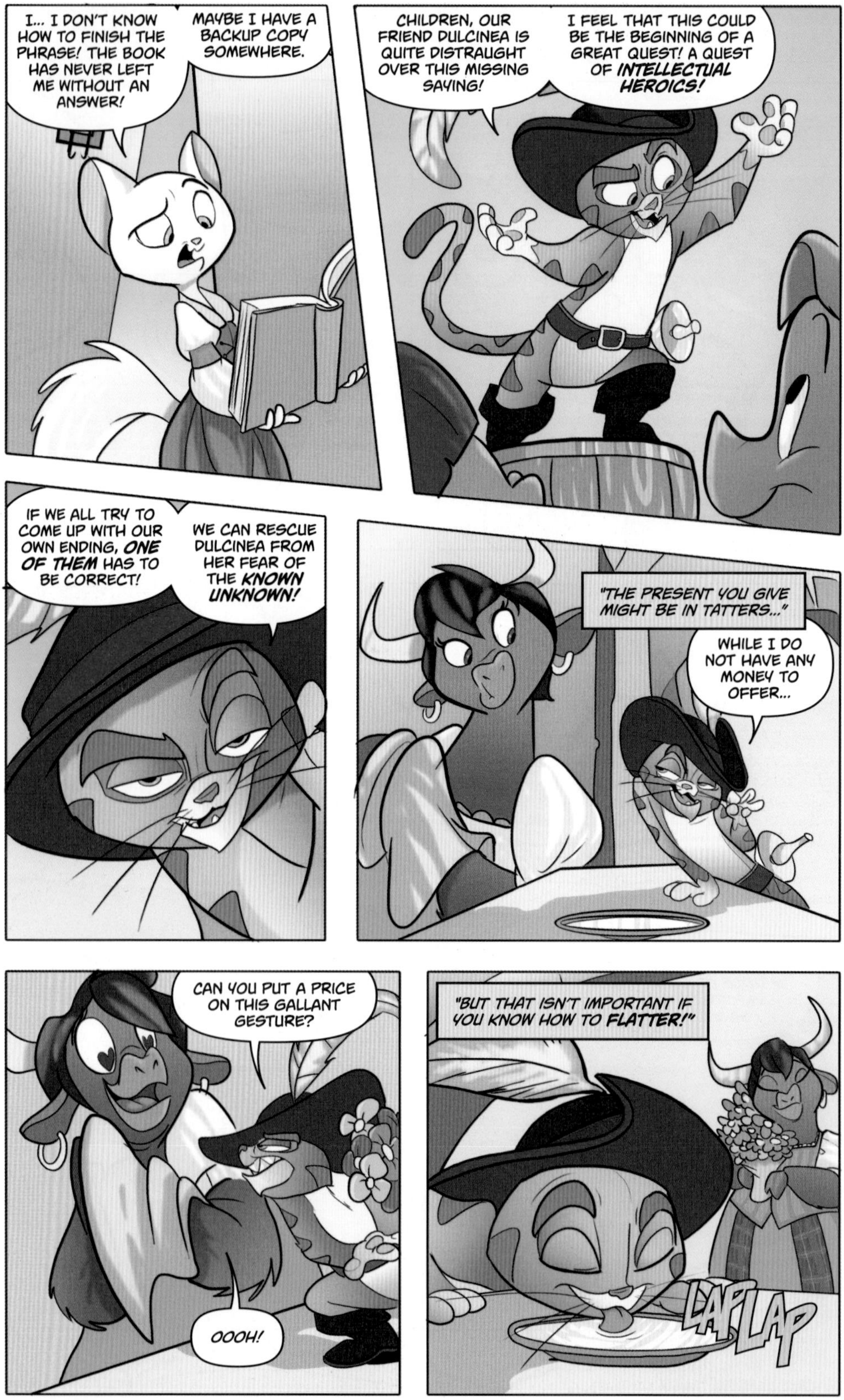
I... I DON'T KNOW HOW TO FINISH THE PHRASE! THE BOOK HAS NEVER LEFT ME WITHOUT AN ANSWER!
MAYBE I HAVE A BACKUP COPY SOMEWHERE.
CHILDREN, OUR FRIEND DULCINEA IS QUITE DISTRAUGHT OVER THIS MISSING SAYING!
I FEEL THAT THIS COULD BE THE BEGINNING OF A GREAT QUEST! A QUEST OF INTELLECTUAL HEROICS!
IF WE ALL TRY TO COME UP WITH OUR OWN ENDING, ONE OF THEM HAS TO BE CORRECT!
WE CAN RESCUE DULCINEA FROM HER FEAR OF THE KNOWN UNKNOWN!
"THE PRESENT YOU GIVE MIGHT BE IN TATTERS..."
WHILE I DO NOT HAVE ANY MONEY TO OFFER...
CAN YOU PUT A PRICE ON THIS GALLANT GESTURE?
OOOH!
"BUT THAT ISN'T IMPORTANT IF YOU KNOW HOW TO FLATTER!"
LAP LAP

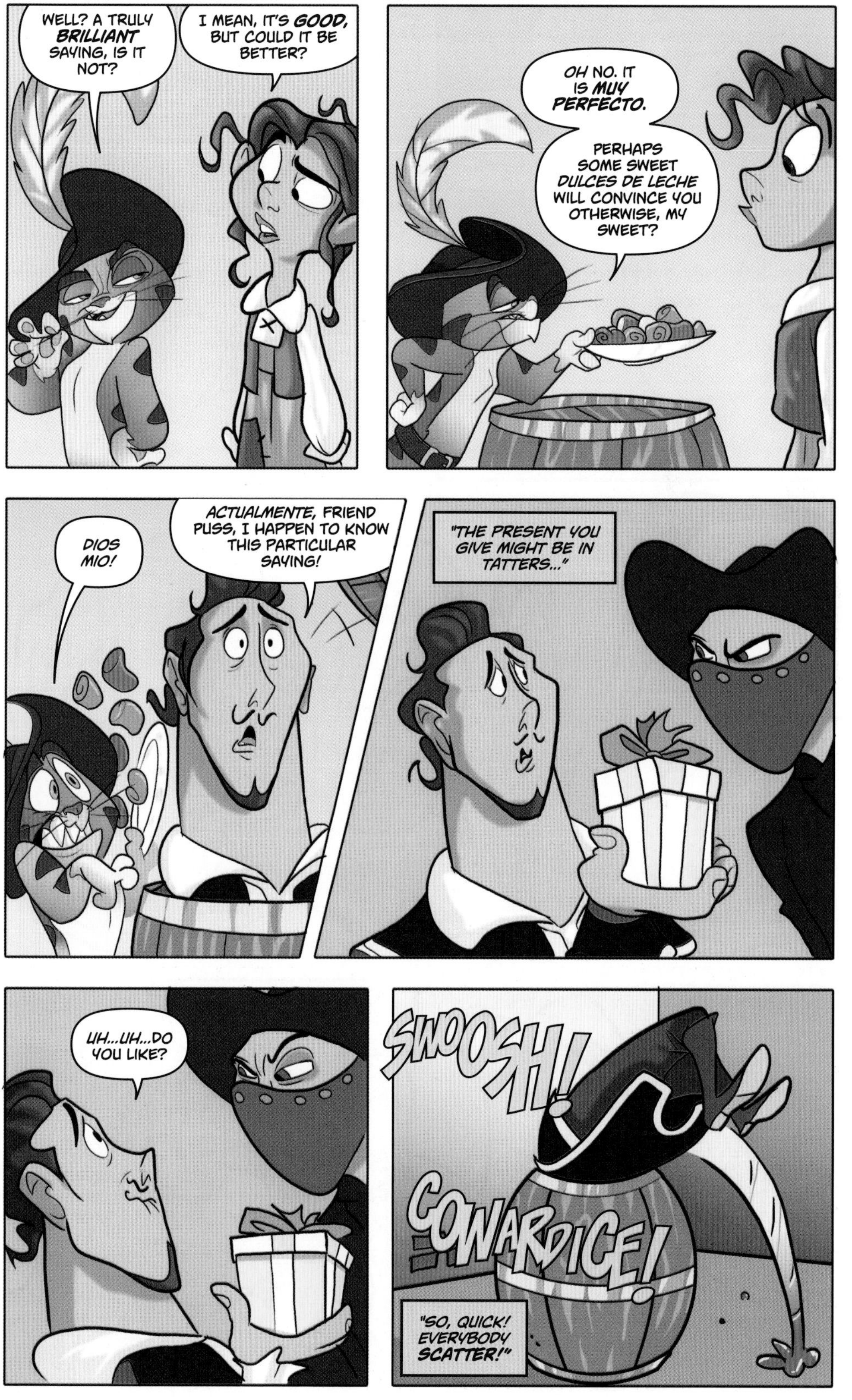
WELL? A TRULY BRILLIANT SAYING, IS IT NOT?
I MEAN, IT'S GOOD, BUT COULD IT BE BETTER?
OH NO. IT IS MUY PERFECTO.
PERHAPS SOME SWEET DULCES DE LECHE WILL CONVINCE YOU OTHERWISE, MY SWEET?
DIOS MIO!
ACTUALMENTE, FRIEND PUSS, I HAPPEN TO KNOW THIS PARTICULAR SAYING!
"THE PRESENT YOU GIVE MIGHT BE IN TATTERS..."
UH...UH...DO YOU LIKE?
SWOOSH!!
COWARDICE!
"SO, QUICK! EVERYBODY SCATTER!"

WELL, I GUESS THAT I'LL TAKE A STAB AT THIS!

CAN'T BE WORSE THAN YOUR ATTEMPT AT A GIFT...

"THE PRESENT YOU GIVE MIGHT BE IN TATTERS..."

HMMM... I NEED A PRESENT THAT *REALLY* REMINDS ME OF CLEEVIL...

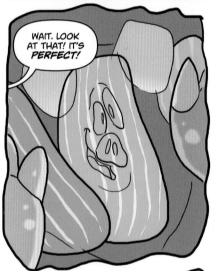

WAIT. LOOK AT THAT! IT'S *PERFECT!*

SHE'S GOING TO LOVE THIS!

"BUT A GOOD FRIEND WILL LOVE IT, AS IF IT'S ON A *GOLDEN PLATTER!*"

I GUESS YOU MAKE A GOOD POINT, TOBY. THANKS FOR THE PRESENT.

EVEN THOUGH I REALLY WANTED A SLINGSHOT...

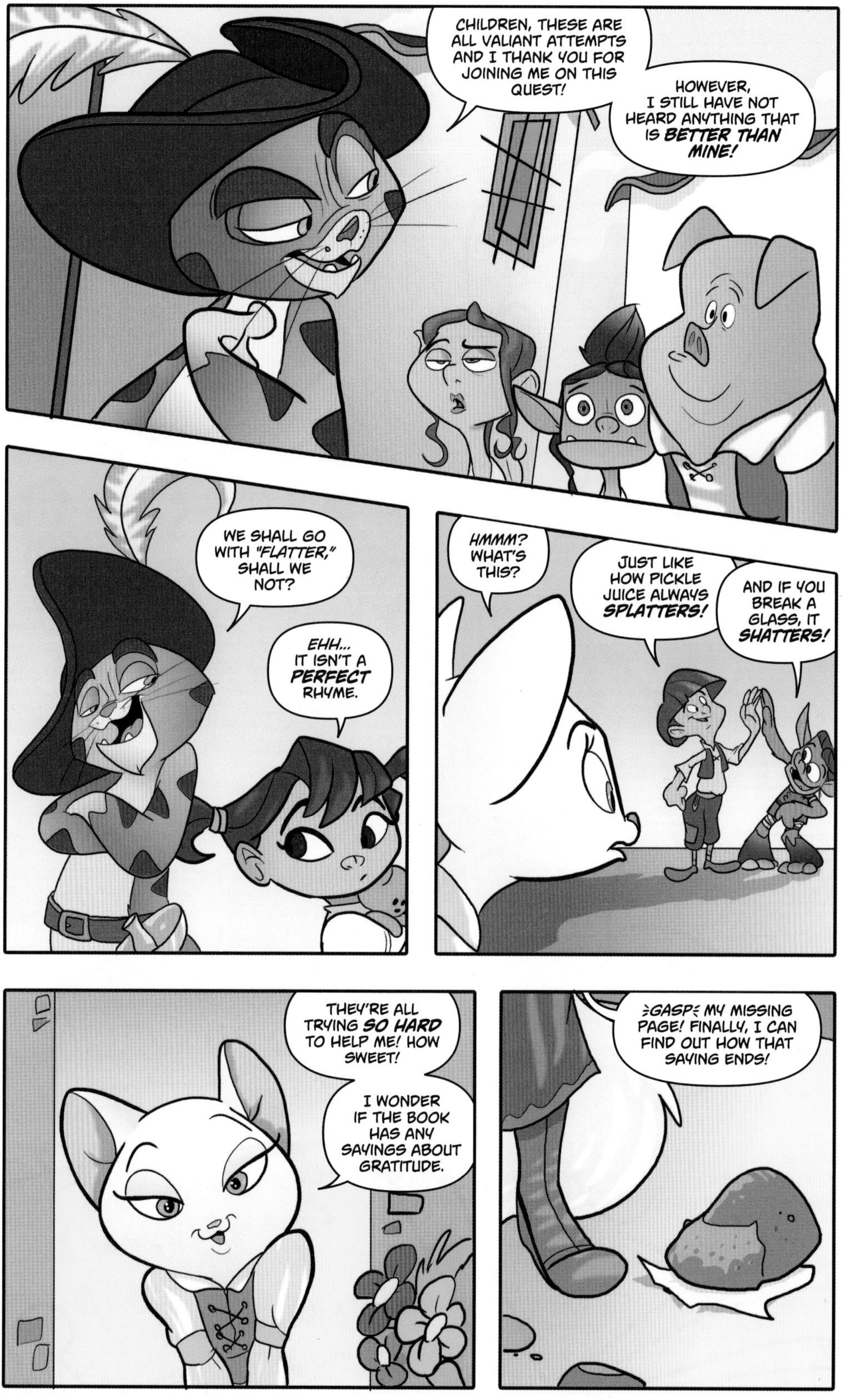
CHILDREN, THESE ARE ALL VALIANT ATTEMPTS AND I THANK YOU FOR JOINING ME ON THIS QUEST!
HOWEVER, I STILL HAVE NOT HEARD ANYTHING THAT IS BETTER THAN MINE!
WE SHALL GO WITH "FLATTER," SHALL WE NOT?
EHH... IT ISN'T A PERFECT RHYME.
HMMM? WHAT'S THIS?
JUST LIKE HOW PICKLE JUICE ALWAYS SPLATTERS!
AND IF YOU BREAK A GLASS, IT SHATTERS!
THEY'RE ALL TRYING SO HARD TO HELP ME! HOW SWEET!
I WONDER IF THE BOOK HAS ANY SAYINGS ABOUT GRATITUDE.
≷GASP≶ MY MISSING PAGE! FINALLY, I CAN FIND OUT HOW THAT SAYING ENDS!

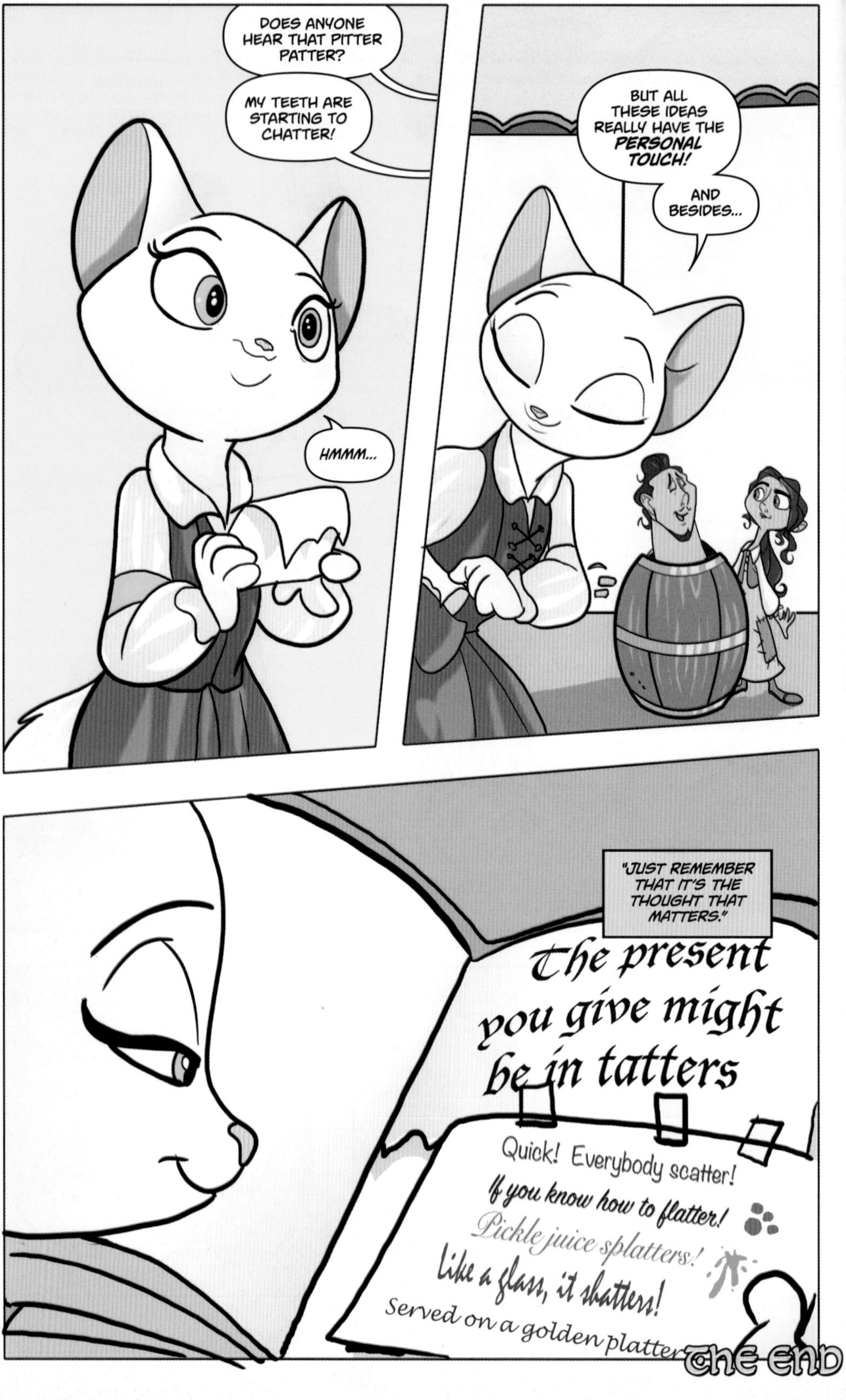
DOES ANYONE HEAR THAT PITTER PATTER?
MY TEETH ARE STARTING TO CHATTER!
HMMM...
BUT ALL THESE IDEAS REALLY HAVE THE **PERSONAL TOUCH!**
AND BESIDES...
"JUST REMEMBER THAT IT'S THE THOUGHT THAT MATTERS."
The present you give might be in tatters
Quick! Everybody scatter!
If you know how to flatter!
Pickle juice splatters!
Like a glass, it shatters!
Served on a golden platter
THE END

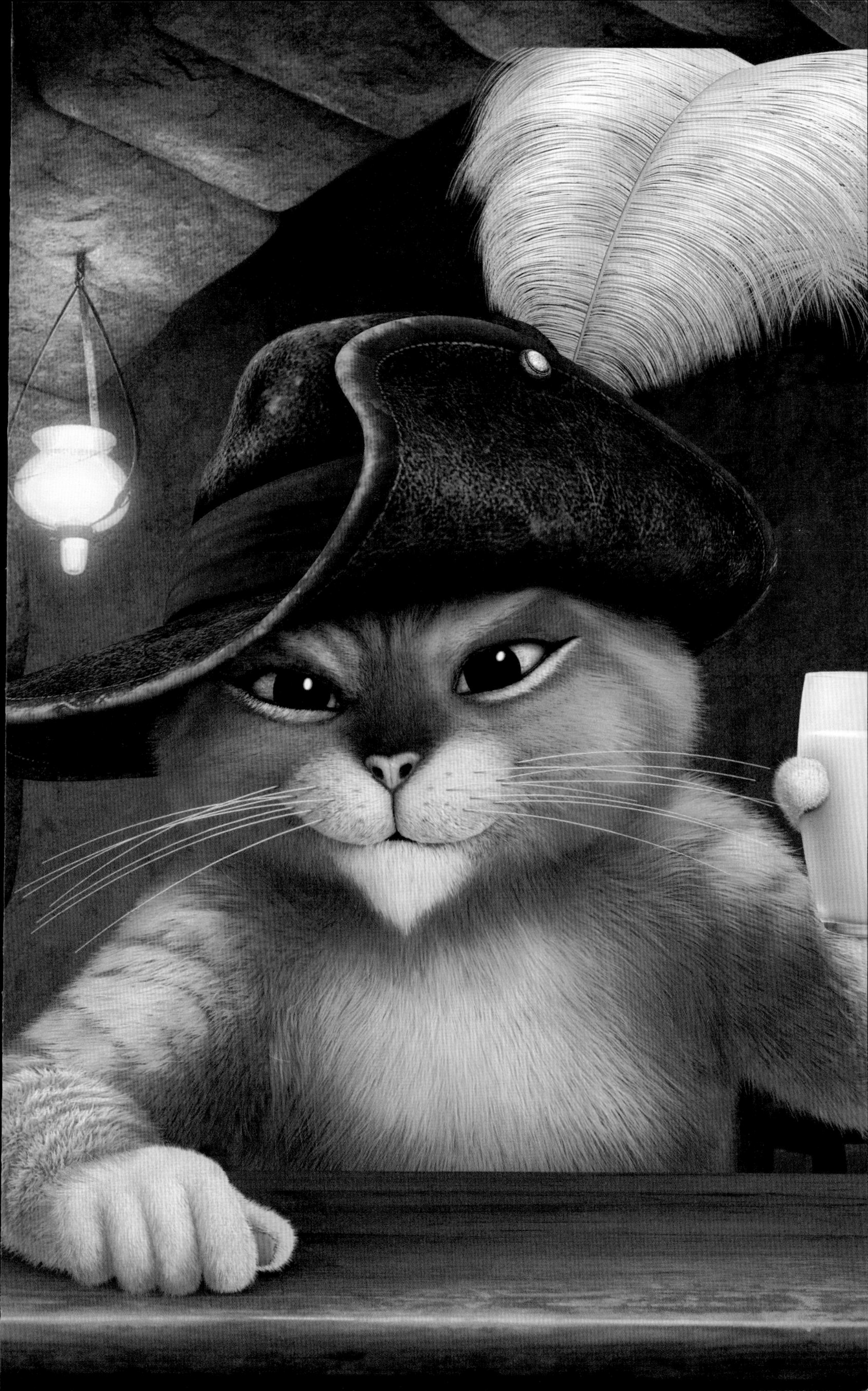

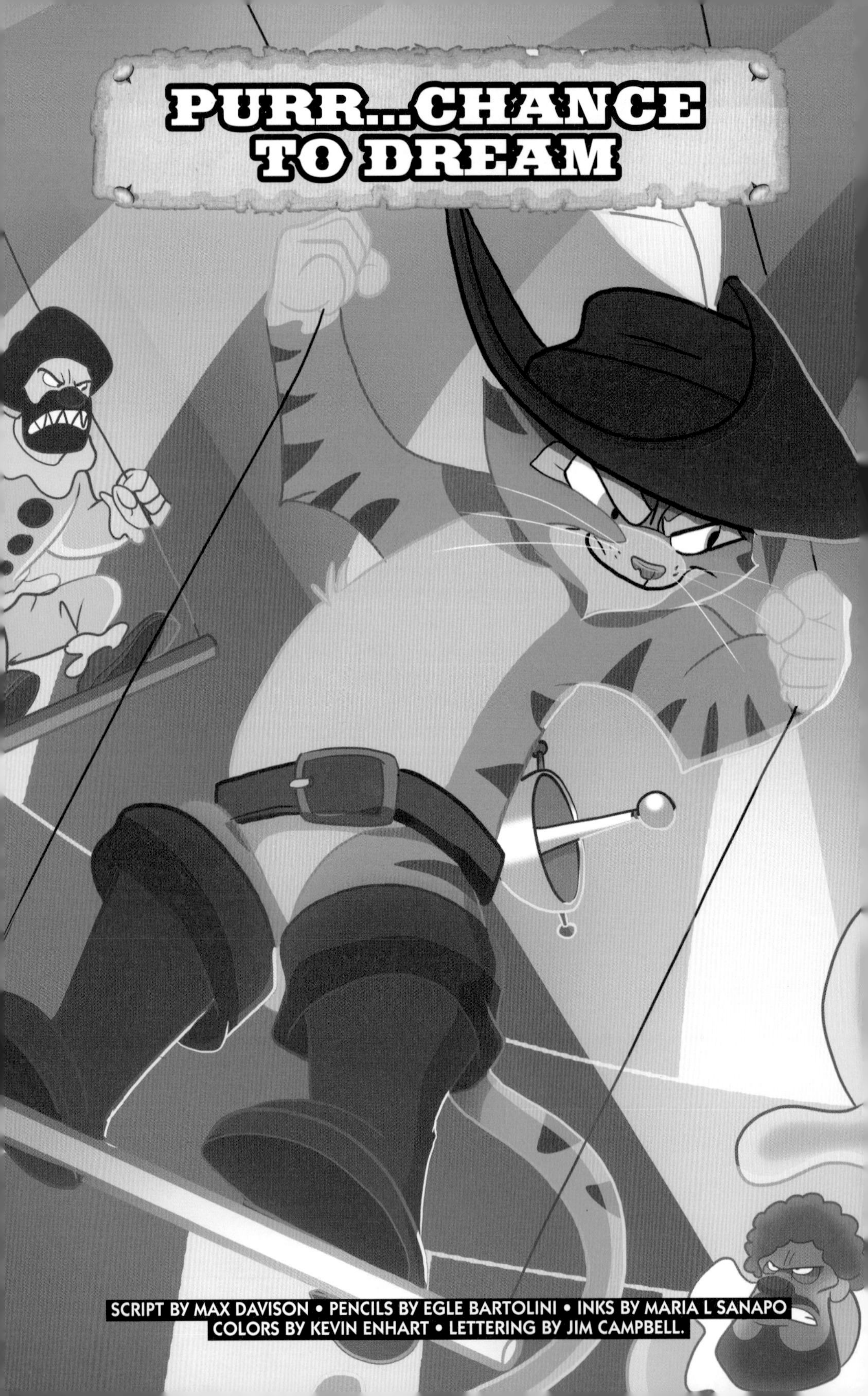
PURR...CHANCE TO DREAM
SCRIPT BY MAX DAVISON • PENCILS BY EGLE BARTOLINI • INKS BY MARIA L SANAPO
COLORS BY KEVIN ENHART • LETTERING BY JIM CAMPBELL.

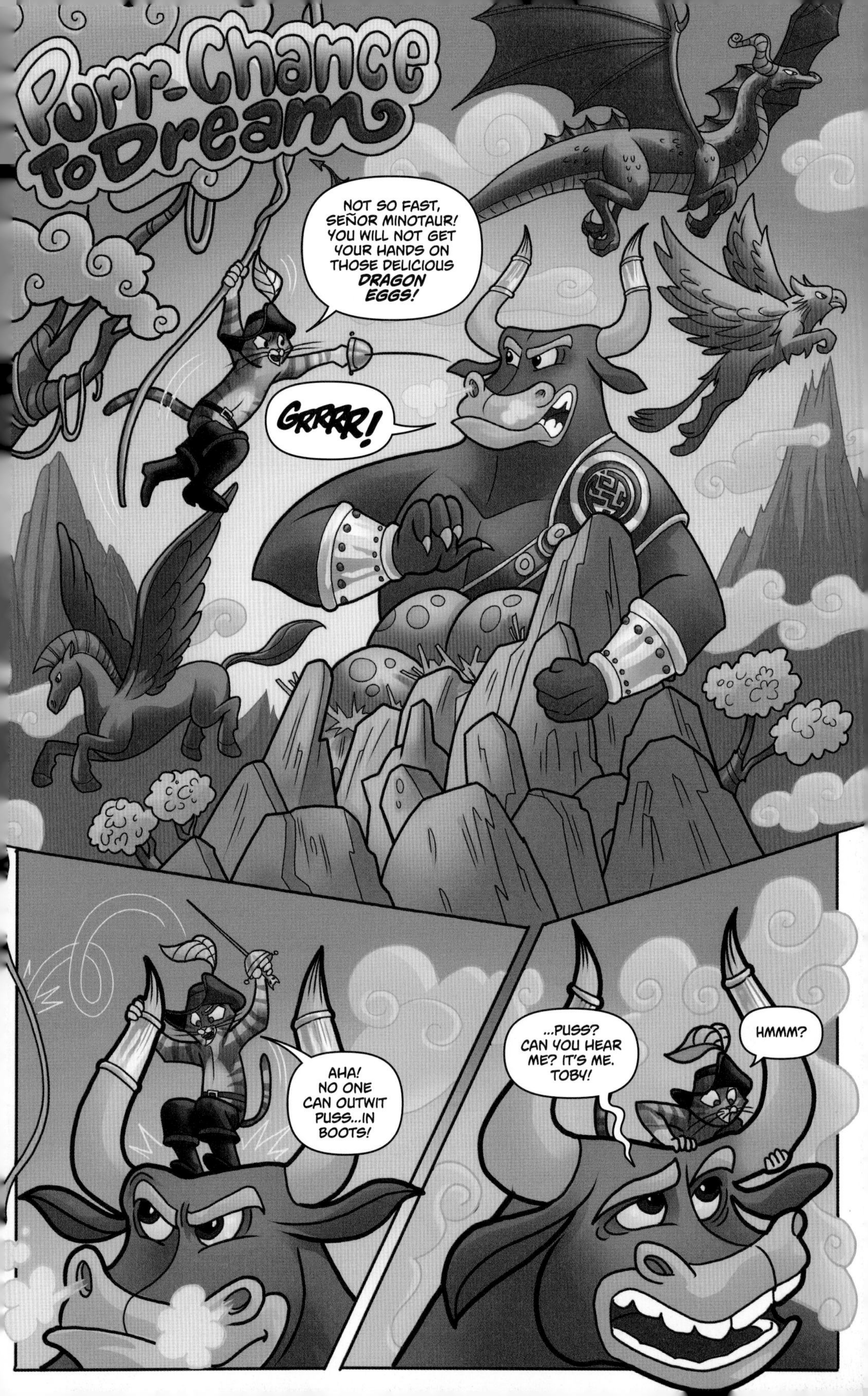
Purr-Chance To Dream
NOT SO FAST, SEÑOR MINOTAUR! YOU WILL NOT GET YOUR HANDS ON THOSE DELICIOUS DRAGON EGGS!
GRRRR!
AHA! NO ONE CAN OUTWIT PUSS...IN BOOTS!
...PUSS? CAN YOU HEAR ME? IT'S ME. TOBY!
HMMM?

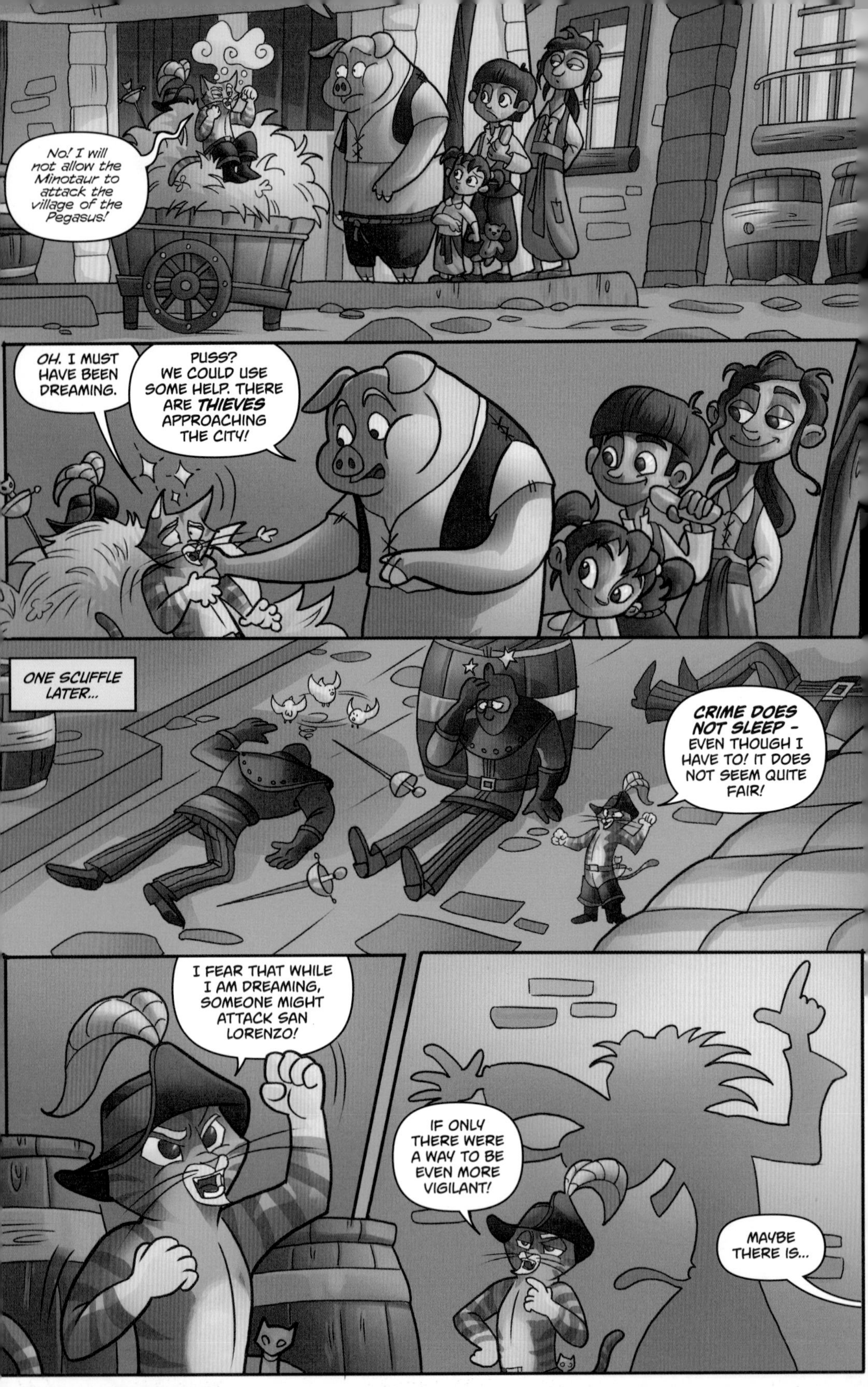

No! I will not allow the Minotaur to attack the village of the Pegasus!
OH. I MUST HAVE BEEN DREAMING.
PUSS? WE COULD USE SOME HELP. THERE ARE THIEVES APPROACHING THE CITY!
ONE SCUFFLE LATER...
CRIME DOES NOT SLEEP - EVEN THOUGH I HAVE TO! IT DOES NOT SEEM QUITE FAIR!
I FEAR THAT WHILE I AM DREAMING, SOMEONE MIGHT ATTACK SAN LORENZO!
IF ONLY THERE WERE A WAY TO BE EVEN MORE VIGILANT!
MAYBE THERE IS...

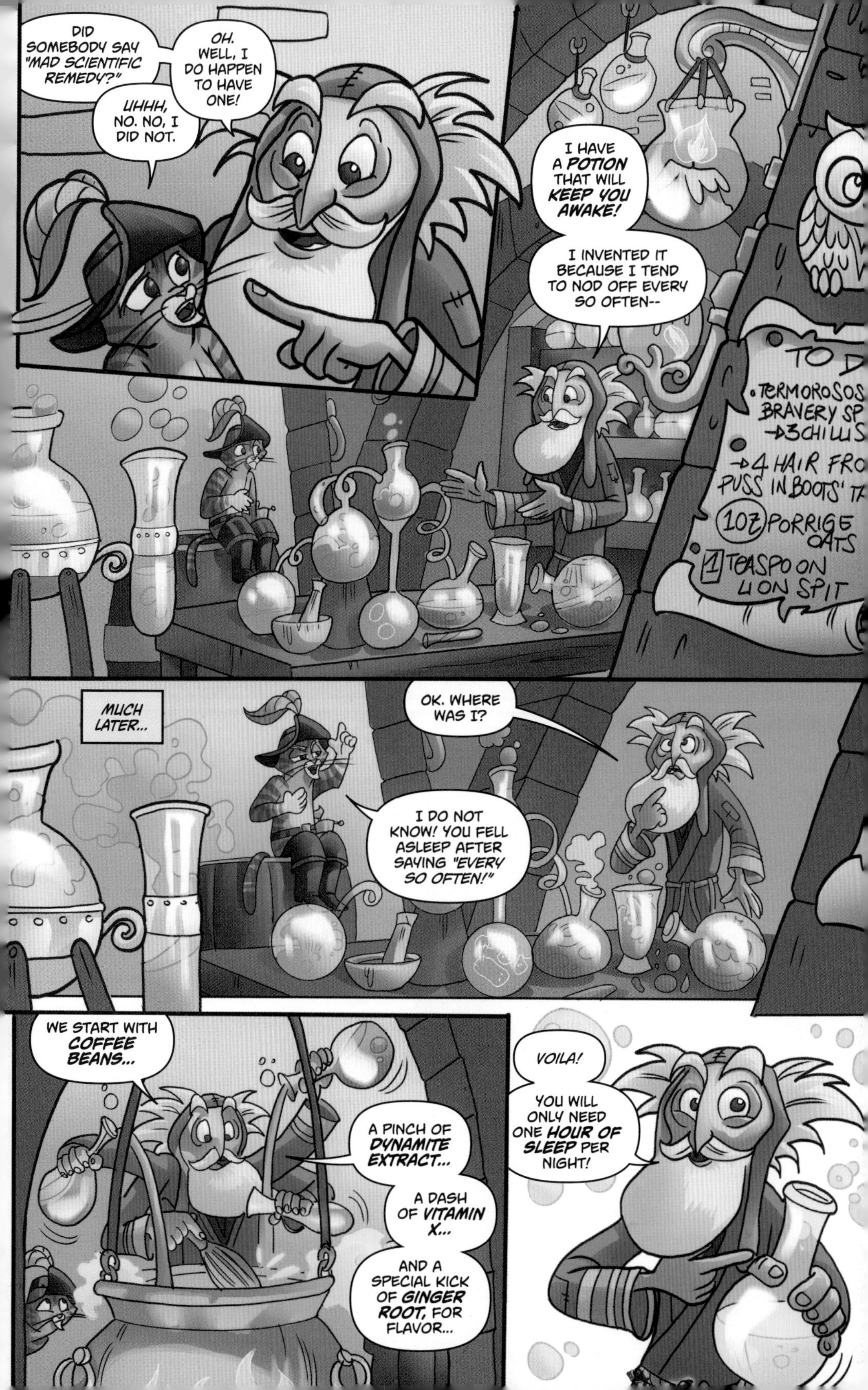

DID SOMEBODY SAY "MAD SCIENTIFIC REMEDY?"
UHHH, NO. NO, I DID NOT.
OH. WELL, I DO HAPPEN TO HAVE ONE!
I HAVE A POTION THAT WILL KEEP YOU AWAKE!
I INVENTED IT BECAUSE I TEND TO NOD OFF EVERY SO OFTEN--
TO D
TERMOROSOS BRAVERY SP
→3 CHILLIS
→4 HAIR FRO PUSS IN BOOTS' TA
1OZ PORRIGE OATS
1 TEASPOON LION SPIT
MUCH LATER...
OK. WHERE WAS I?
I DO NOT KNOW! YOU FELL ASLEEP AFTER SAYING "EVERY SO OFTEN!"
WE START WITH COFFEE BEANS...
A PINCH OF DYNAMITE EXTRACT...
A DASH OF VITAMIN X...
AND A SPECIAL KICK OF GINGER ROOT, FOR FLAVOR...
VOILA!
YOU WILL ONLY NEED ONE HOUR OF SLEEP PER NIGHT!

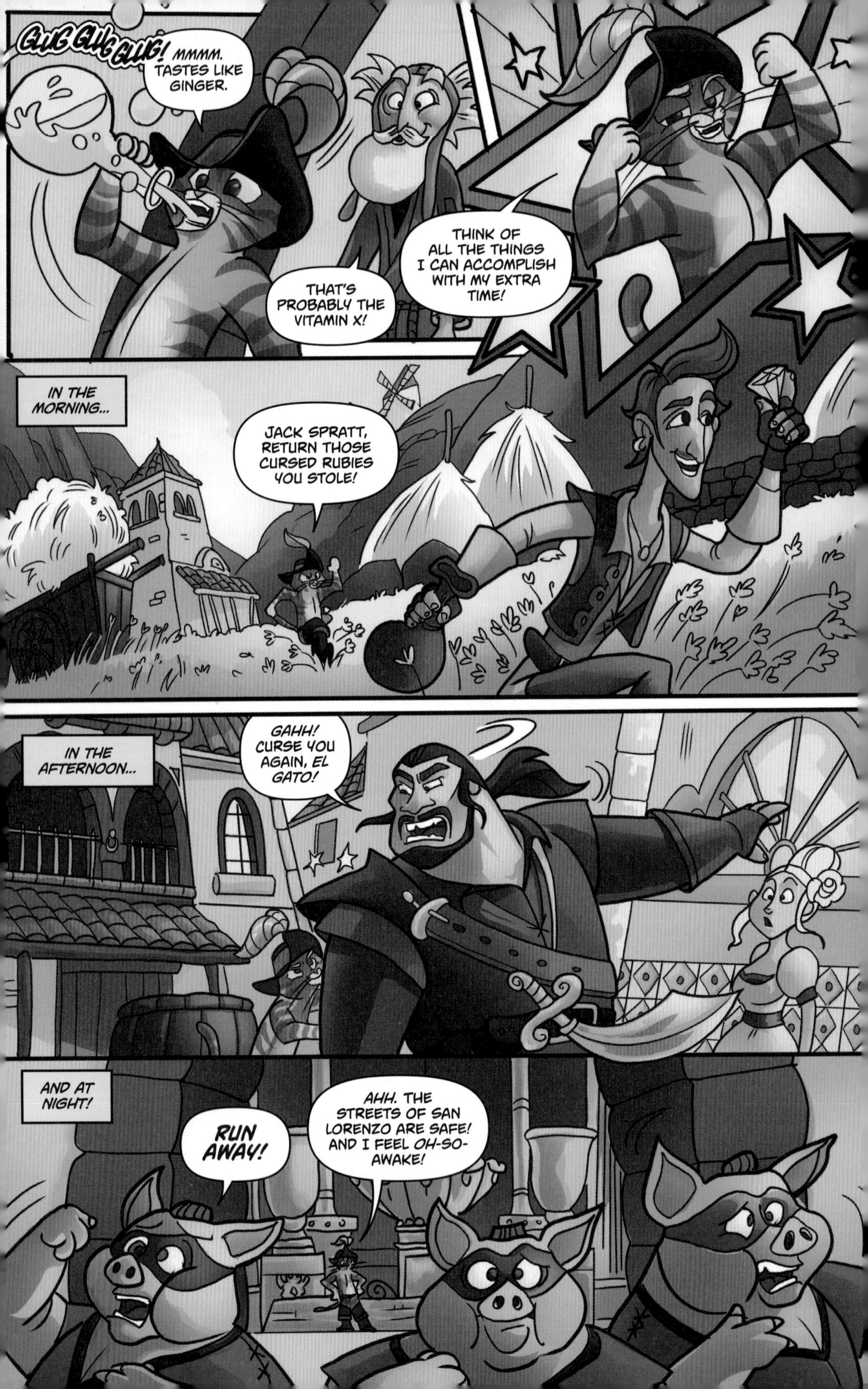
GLUG GLUG GLUG!
MMMM. TASTES LIKE GINGER.
THAT'S PROBABLY THE VITAMIN X!
THINK OF ALL THE THINGS I CAN ACCOMPLISH WITH MY EXTRA TIME!
IN THE MORNING...
JACK SPRATT, RETURN THOSE CURSED RUBIES YOU STOLE!
IN THE AFTERNOON...
GAHH! CURSE YOU AGAIN, EL GATO!
AND AT NIGHT!
RUN AWAY!
AHH. THE STREETS OF SAN LORENZO ARE SAFE! AND I FEEL OH-SO-AWAKE!

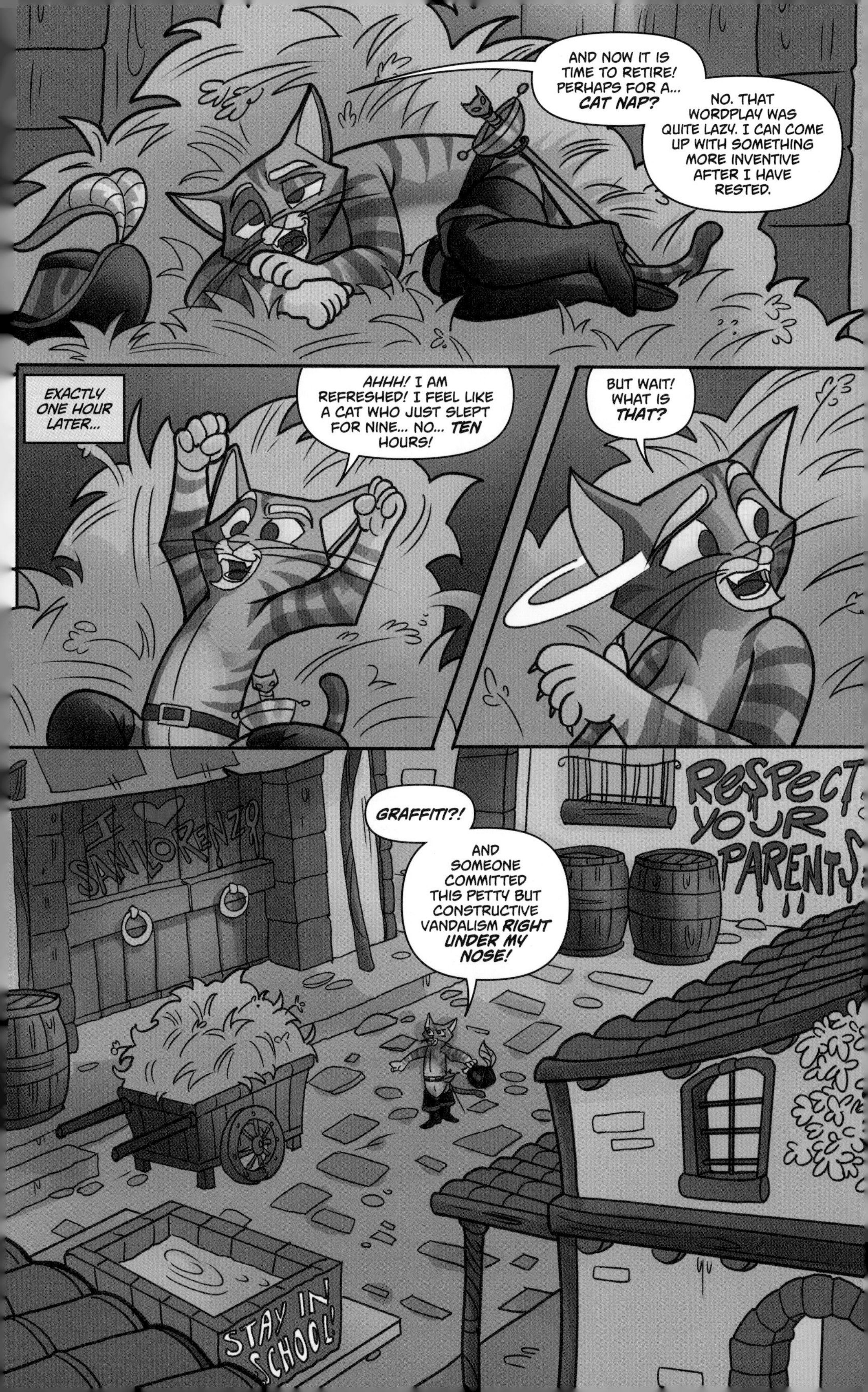
AND NOW IT IS TIME TO RETIRE! PERHAPS FOR A... **CAT NAP?**
NO. THAT WORDPLAY WAS QUITE LAZY. I CAN COME UP WITH SOMETHING MORE INVENTIVE AFTER I HAVE RESTED.
EXACTLY ONE HOUR LATER...
AHHH! I AM REFRESHED! I FEEL LIKE A CAT WHO JUST SLEPT FOR NINE... NO... **TEN** HOURS!
BUT WAIT! WHAT IS **THAT?**
GRAFFITI?!
AND SOMEONE COMMITTED THIS PETTY BUT CONSTRUCTIVE VANDALISM **RIGHT UNDER MY NOSE!**
I ♥ SAN LORENZO
RESPECT YOUR PARENTS
STAY IN SCHOOL!

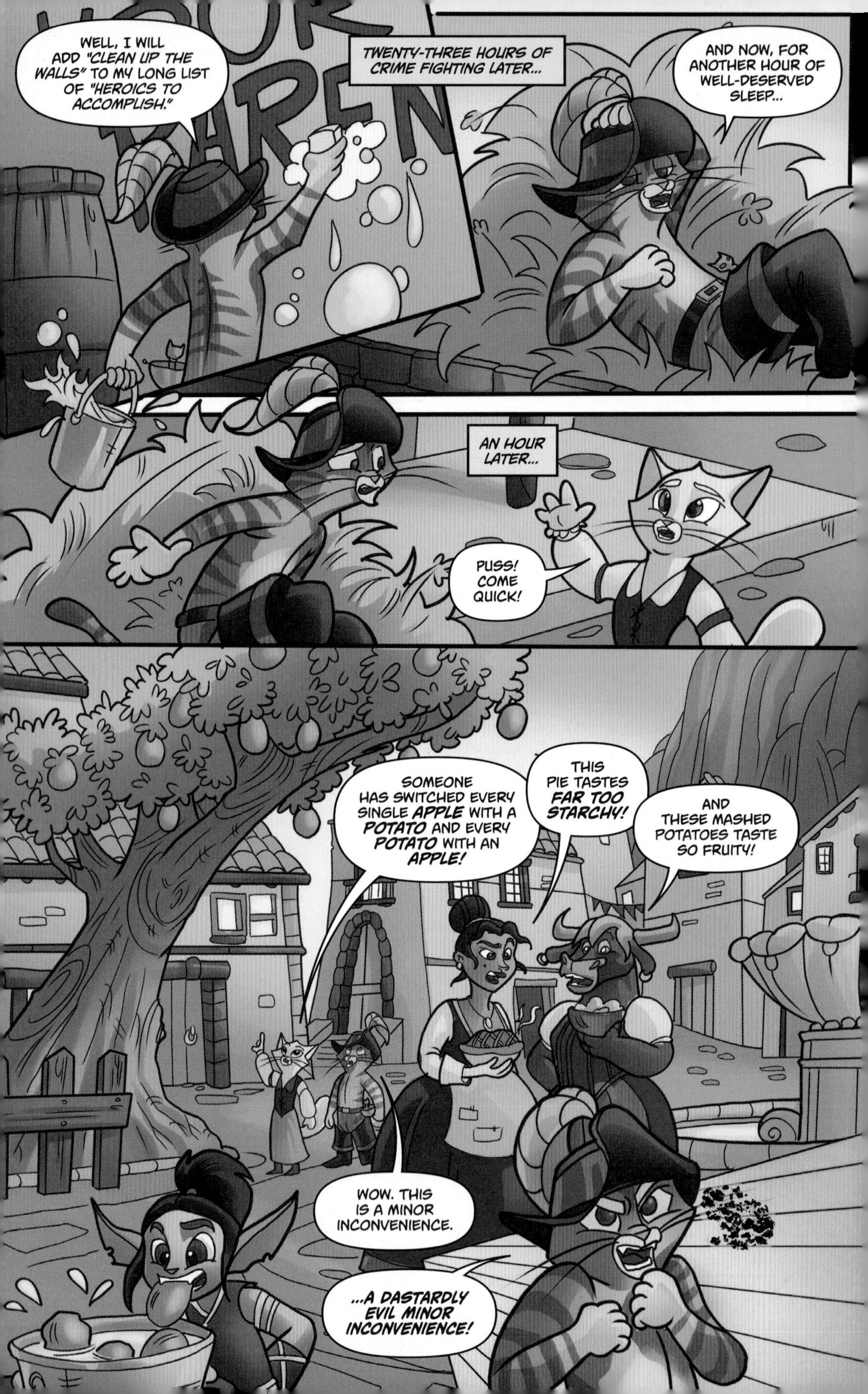

WELL, I WILL ADD "CLEAN UP THE WALLS" TO MY LONG LIST OF "HEROICS TO ACCOMPLISH."
TWENTY-THREE HOURS OF CRIME FIGHTING LATER...
AND NOW, FOR ANOTHER HOUR OF WELL-DESERVED SLEEP...
AN HOUR LATER...
PUSS! COME QUICK!
SOMEONE HAS SWITCHED EVERY SINGLE APPLE WITH A POTATO AND EVERY POTATO WITH AN APPLE!
THIS PIE TASTES FAR TOO STARCHY!
AND THESE MASHED POTATOES TASTE SO FRUITY!
WOW. THIS IS A MINOR INCONVENIENCE.
...A DASTARDLY EVIL MINOR INCONVENIENCE!

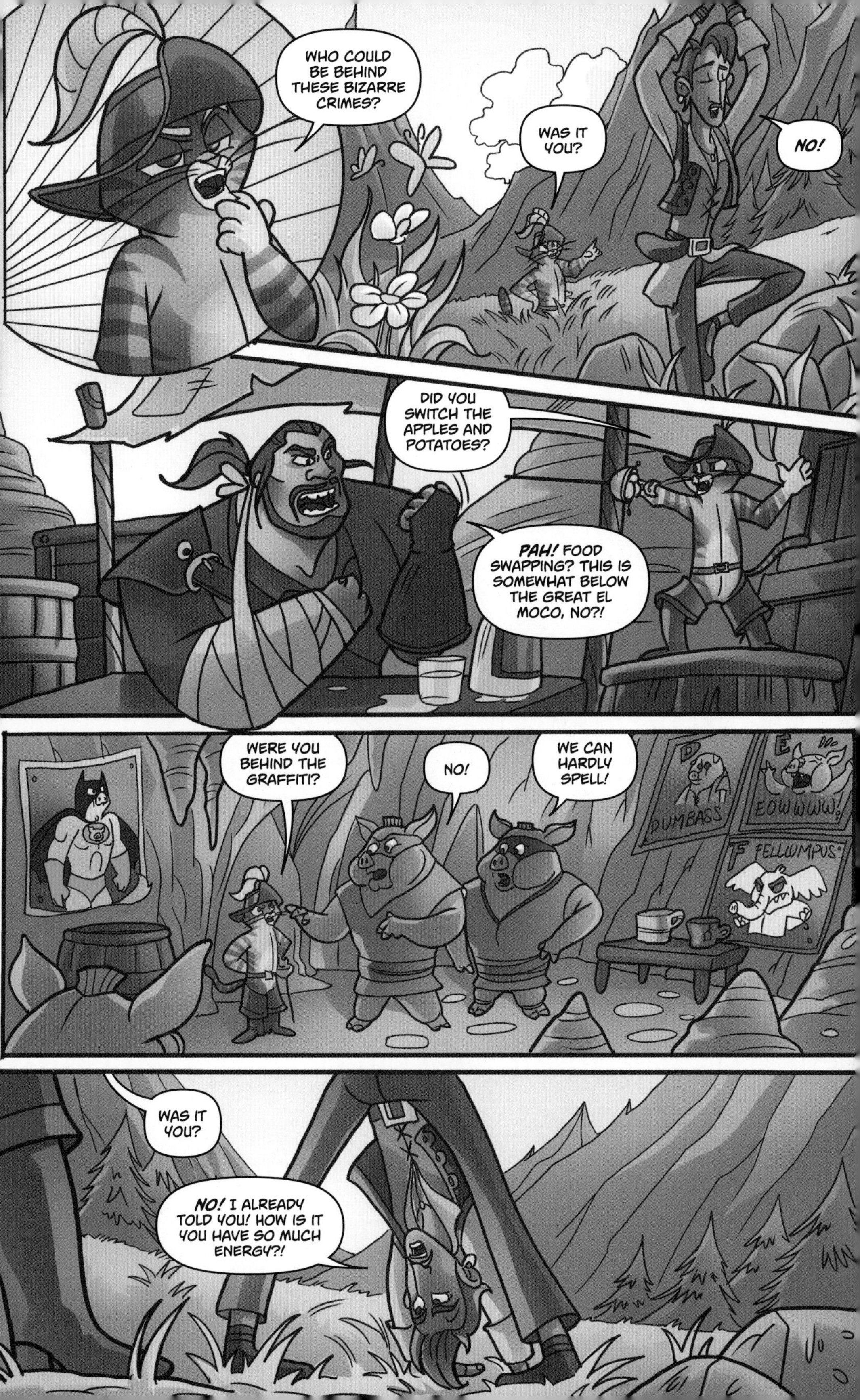
WHO COULD BE BEHIND THESE BIZARRE CRIMES?
WAS IT YOU?
NO!
DID YOU SWITCH THE APPLES AND POTATOES?
PAH! FOOD SWAPPING? THIS IS SOMEWHAT BELOW THE GREAT EL MOCO, NO?!
WERE YOU BEHIND THE GRAFFITI?
NO!
WE CAN HARDLY SPELL!
DUMBASS
EOWWWW!
FELLWUMPUS
WAS IT YOU?
NO! I ALREADY TOLD YOU! HOW IS IT YOU HAVE SO MUCH ENERGY?!

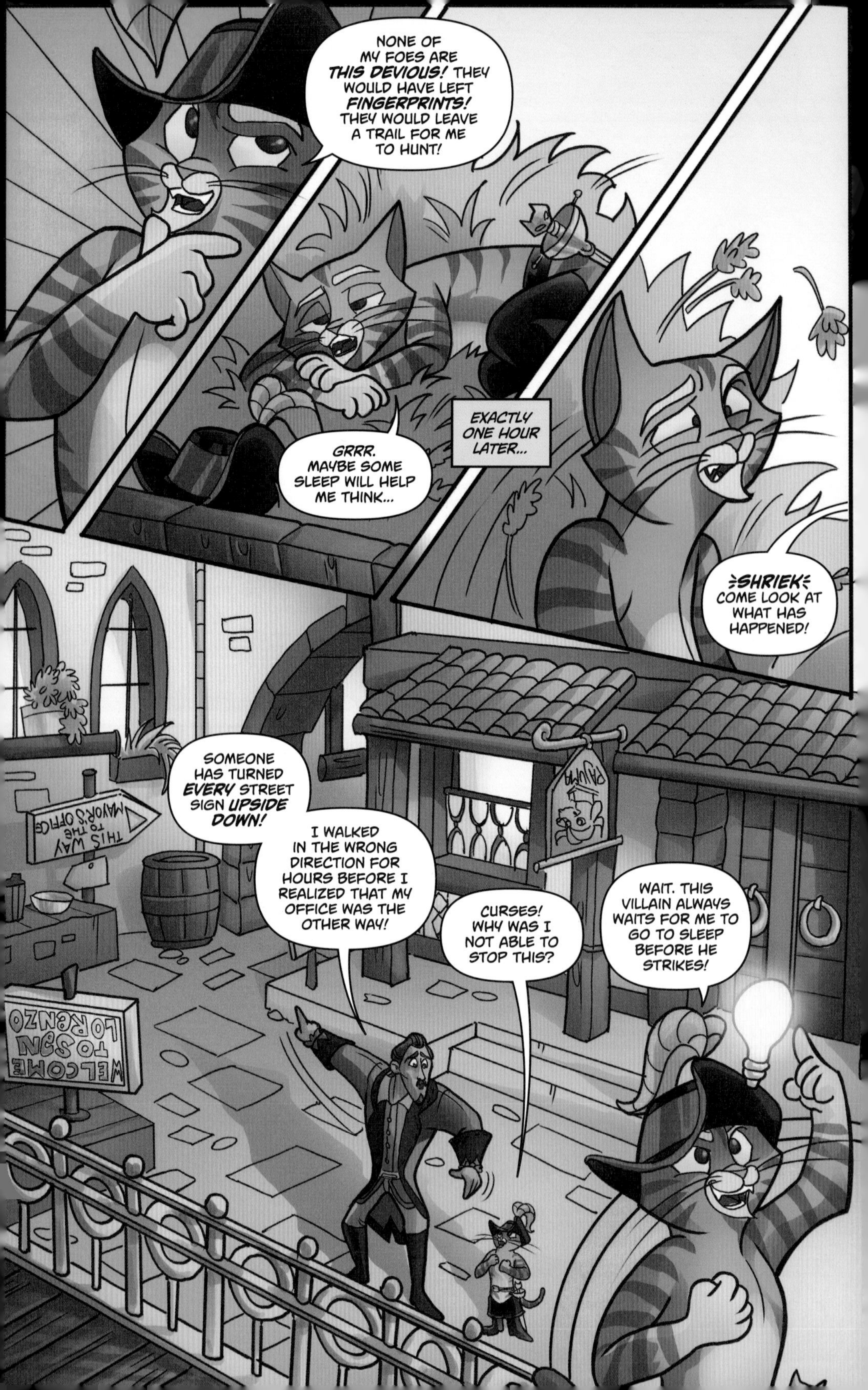

NONE OF MY FOES ARE **THIS DEVIOUS!** THEY WOULD HAVE LEFT **FINGERPRINTS!** THEY WOULD LEAVE A TRAIL FOR ME TO HUNT!
GRRR. MAYBE SOME SLEEP WILL HELP ME THINK...
EXACTLY ONE HOUR LATER...
SHRIEK
COME LOOK AT WHAT HAS HAPPENED!
SOMEONE HAS TURNED **EVERY** STREET SIGN **UPSIDE DOWN!**
I WALKED IN THE WRONG DIRECTION FOR HOURS BEFORE I REALIZED THAT MY OFFICE WAS THE OTHER WAY!
CURSES! WHY WAS I NOT ABLE TO STOP THIS?
WAIT. THIS VILLAIN ALWAYS WAITS FOR ME TO GO TO SLEEP BEFORE HE STRIKES!

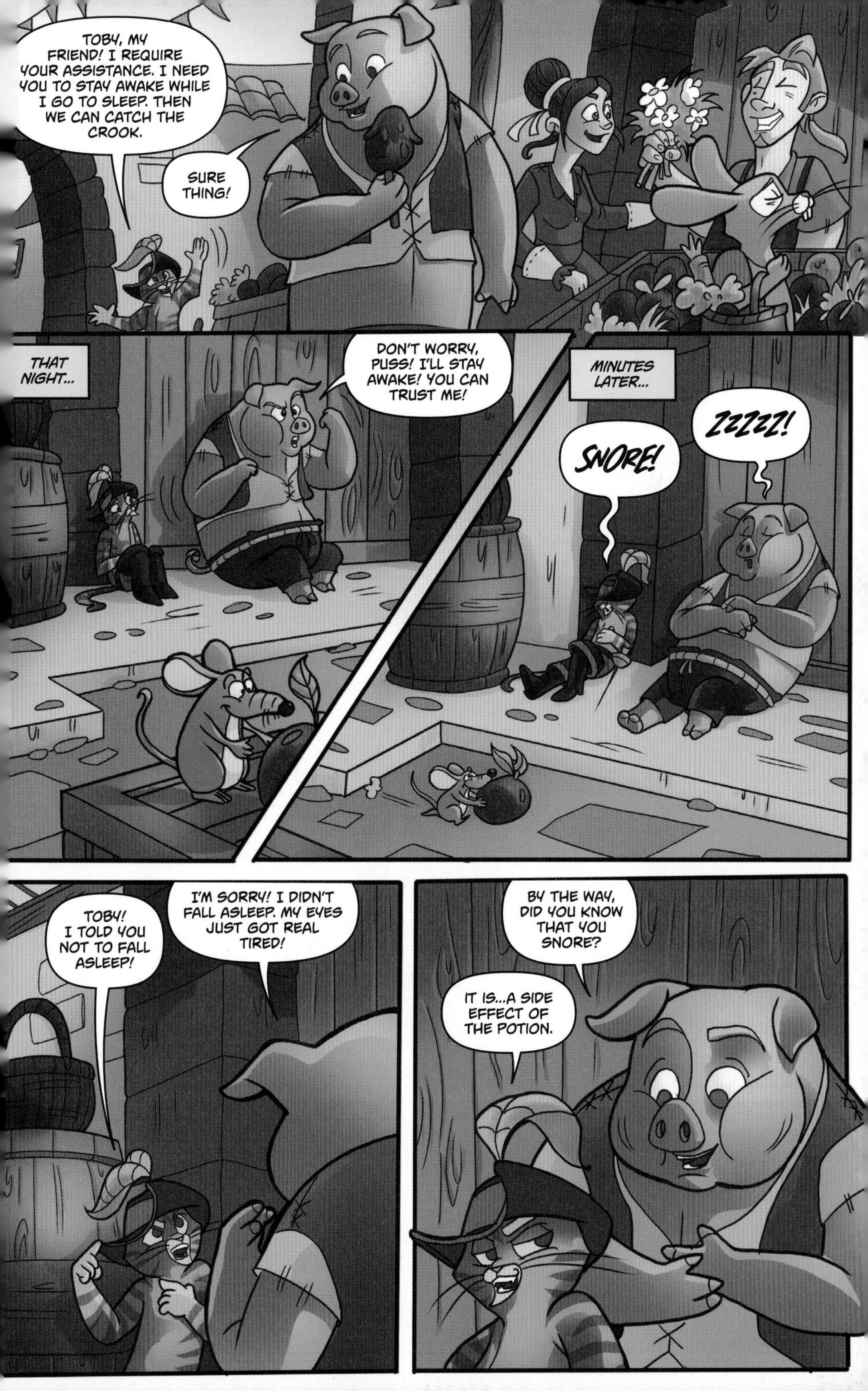
TOBY, MY FRIEND! I REQUIRE YOUR ASSISTANCE. I NEED YOU TO STAY AWAKE WHILE I GO TO SLEEP. THEN WE CAN CATCH THE CROOK.
SURE THING!
THAT NIGHT...
DON'T WORRY, PUSS! I'LL STAY AWAKE! YOU CAN TRUST ME!
MINUTES LATER...
SNORE!
ZZZZZ!
TOBY! I TOLD YOU NOT TO FALL ASLEEP!
I'M SORRY! I DIDN'T FALL ASLEEP. MY EYES JUST GOT REAL TIRED!
BY THE WAY, DID YOU KNOW THAT YOU SNORE?
IT IS...A SIDE EFFECT OF THE POTION.

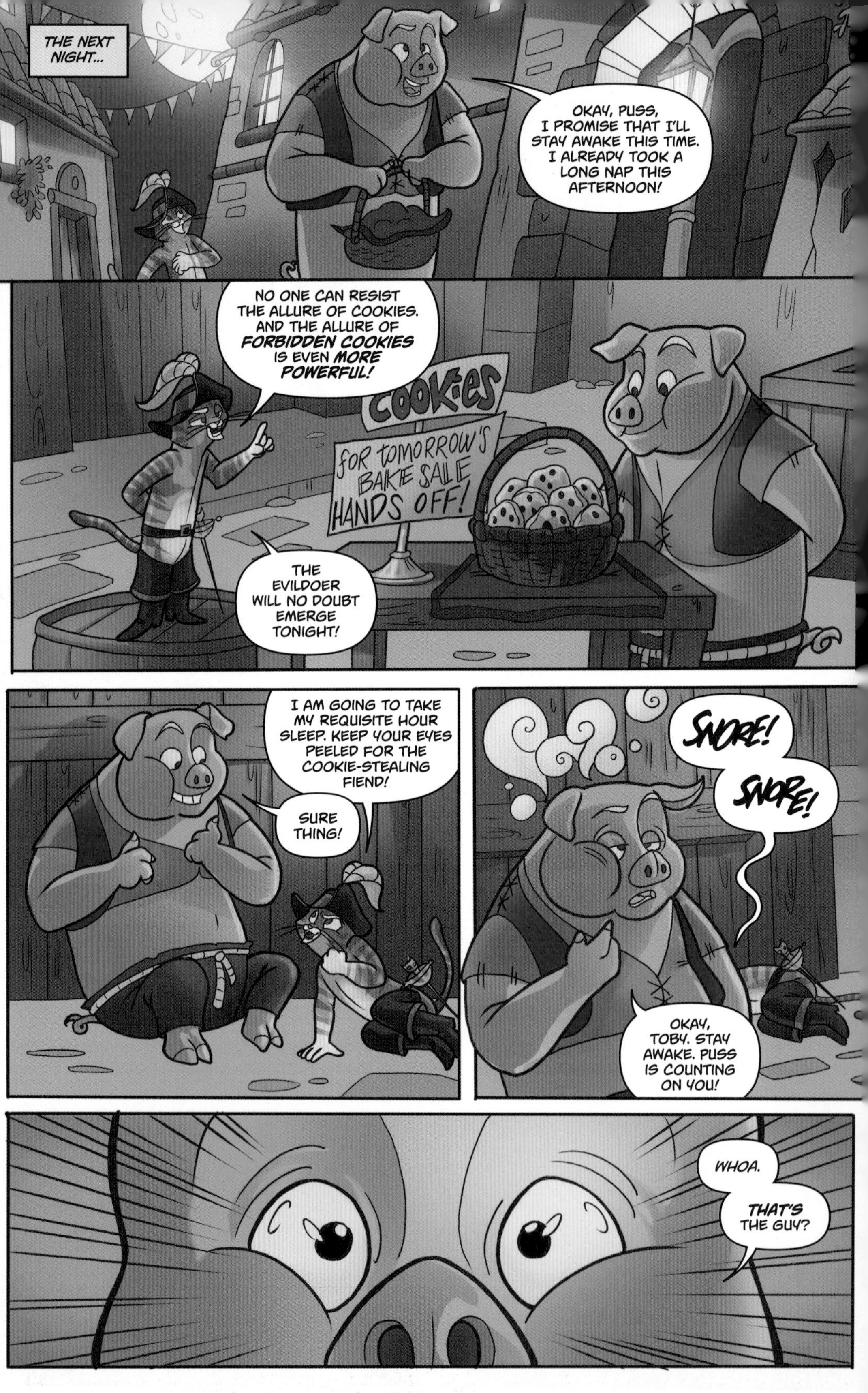
THE NEXT NIGHT...
OKAY, PUSS, I PROMISE THAT I'LL STAY AWAKE THIS TIME. I ALREADY TOOK A LONG NAP THIS AFTERNOON!
NO ONE CAN RESIST THE ALLURE OF COOKIES. AND THE ALLURE OF FORBIDDEN COOKIES IS EVEN MORE POWERFUL!
COOKIES
FOR TOMORROW'S BAKE SALE HANDS OFF!
THE EVILDOER WILL NO DOUBT EMERGE TONIGHT!
I AM GOING TO TAKE MY REQUISITE HOUR SLEEP. KEEP YOUR EYES PEELED FOR THE COOKIE-STEALING FIEND!
SURE THING!
SNORE!
SNORE!
OKAY, TOBY. STAY AWAKE. PUSS IS COUNTING ON YOU!
WHOA.
THAT'S THE GUY?

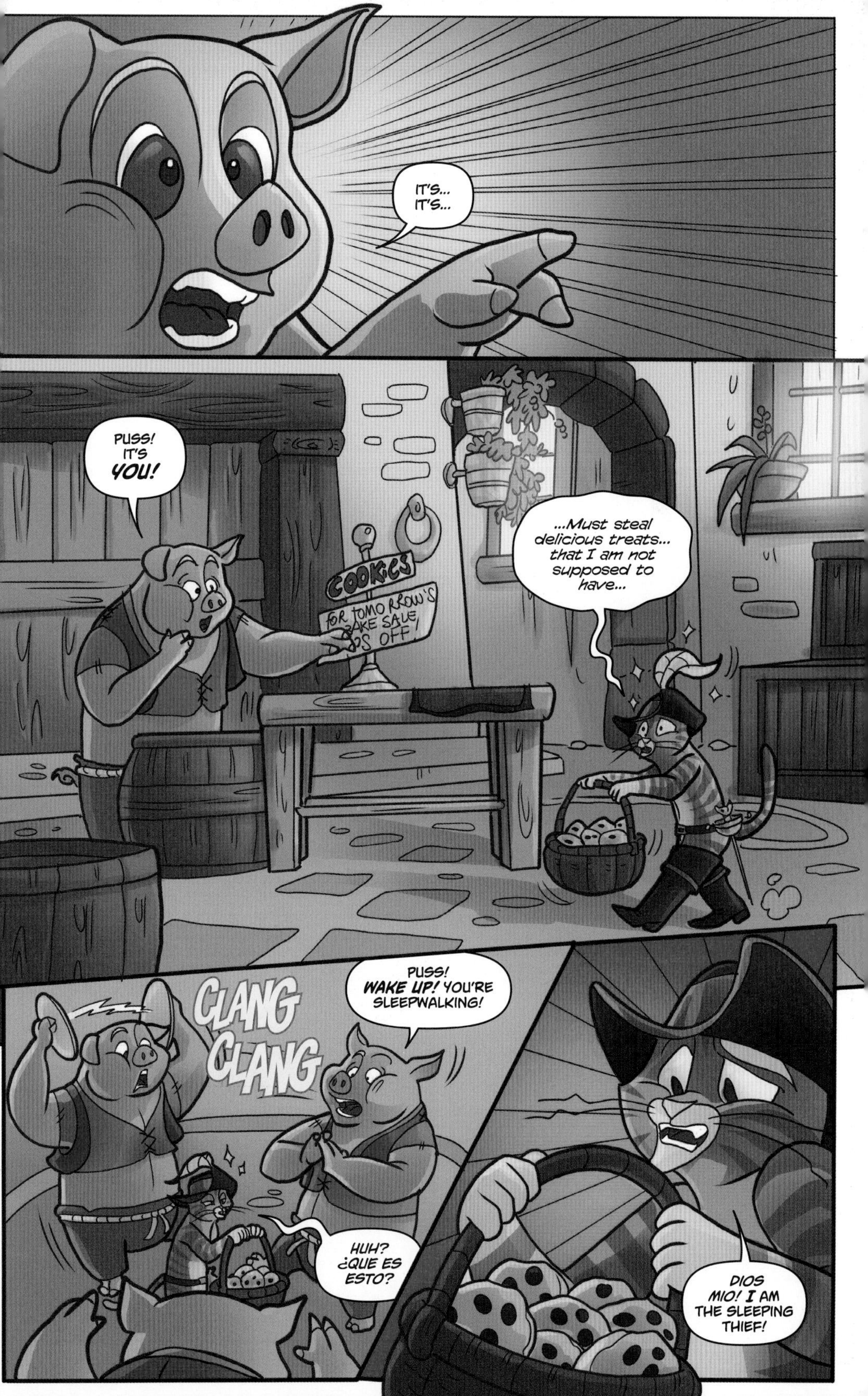
IT'S... IT'S...
PUSS! IT'S **YOU!**
COOKIES
FOR TOMORROW'S
...Must steal delicious treats... that I am not supposed to have...
CLANG CLANG
PUSS! **WAKE UP!** YOU'RE SLEEPWALKING!
HUH? ¿QUE ES ESTO?
DIOS MIO! **I** AM THE SLEEPING THIEF!

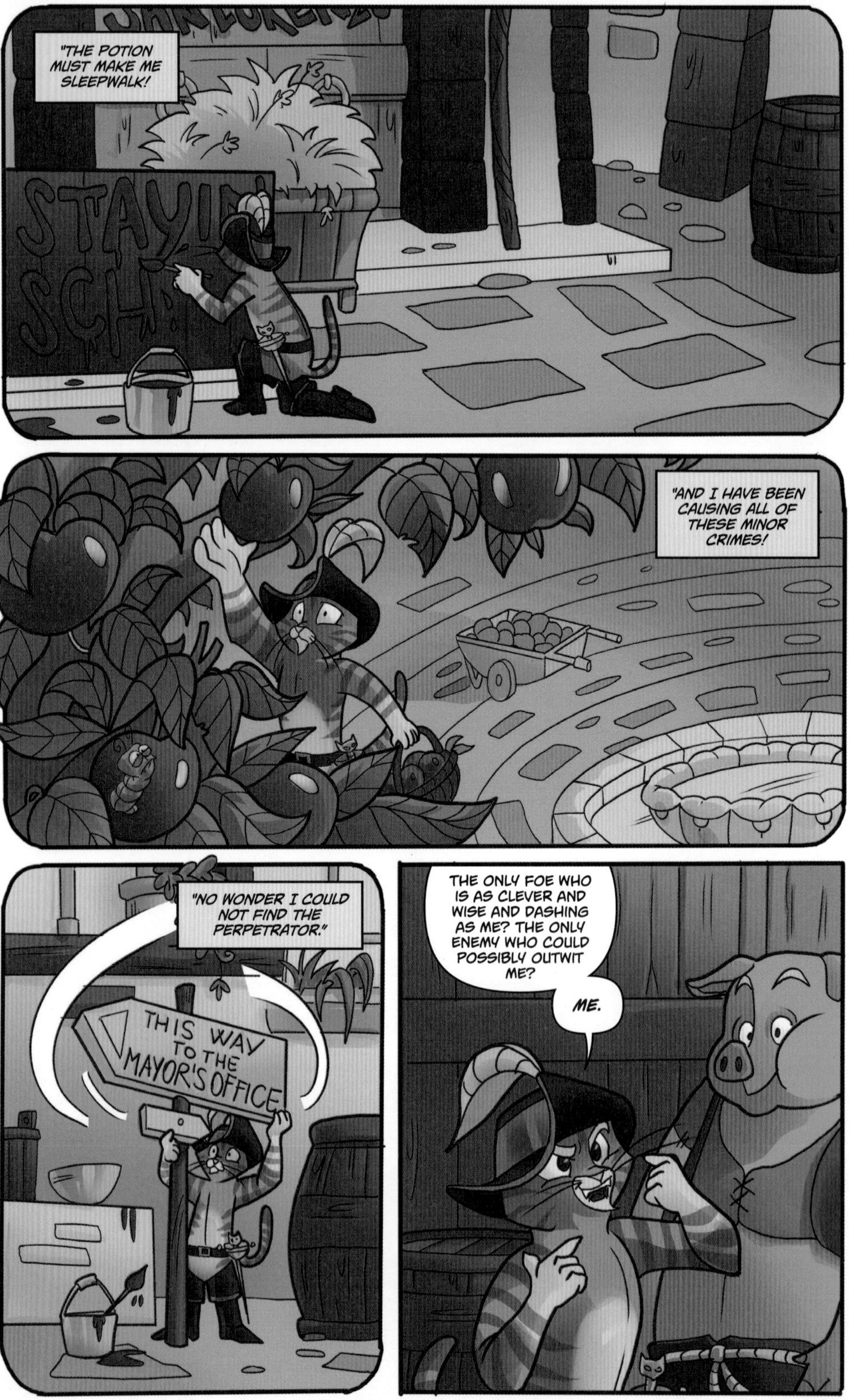

"THE POTION MUST MAKE ME SLEEPWALK!
STAYIN SCH
"AND I HAVE BEEN CAUSING ALL OF THESE MINOR CRIMES!
"NO WONDER I COULD NOT FIND THE PERPETRATOR."
THIS WAY TO THE MAYOR'S OFFICE
THE ONLY FOE WHO IS AS CLEVER AND WISE AND DASHING AS ME? THE ONLY ENEMY WHO COULD POSSIBLY OUTWIT ME?
ME.

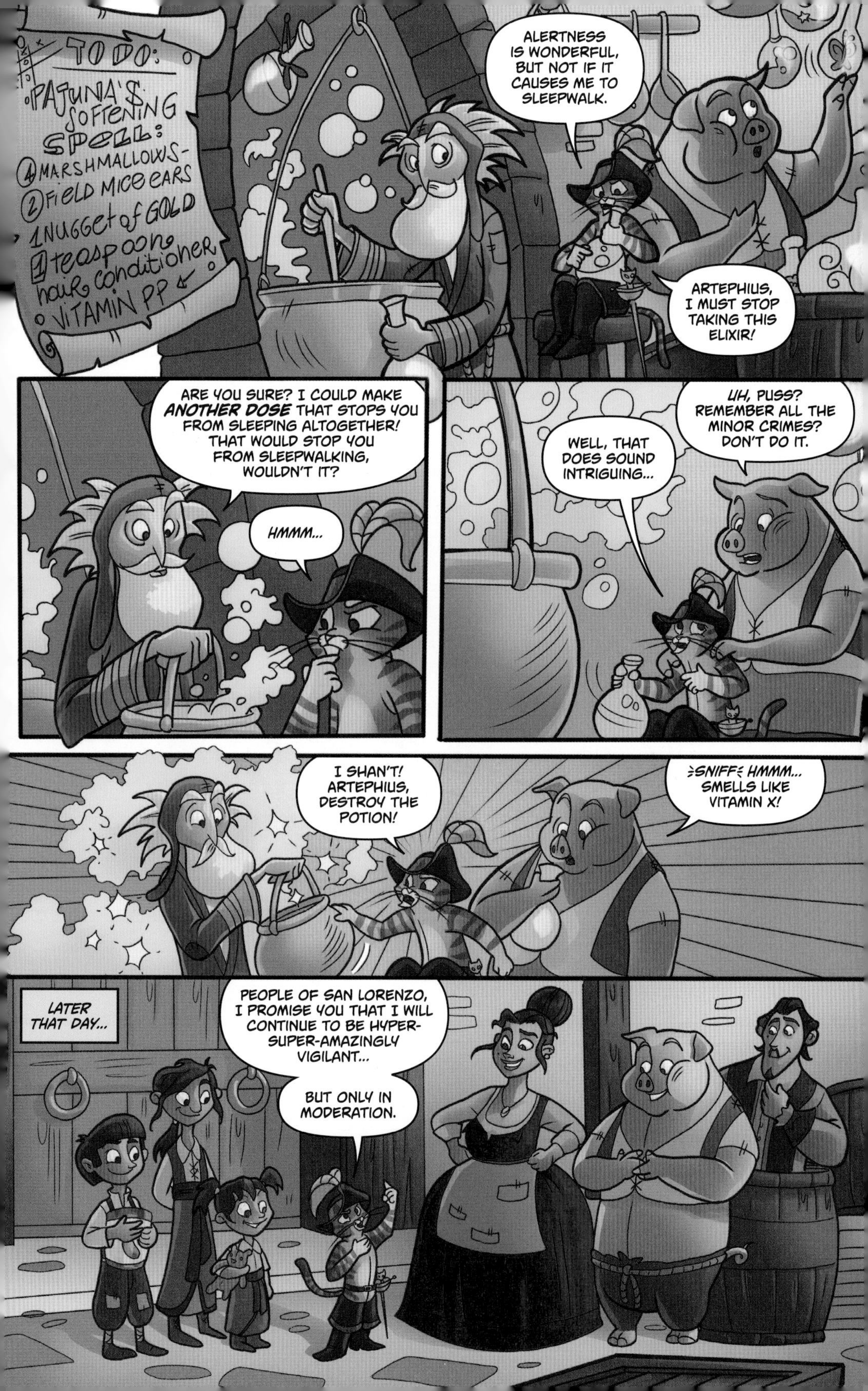

TO DO:
PAJUNA'S SOFTENING SPELL:
4 MARSHMALLOWS-
2 FIELD MICE EARS
1 NUGGET OF GOLD
1 TEASPOON HAIR CONDITIONER
VITAMIN PP
ALERTNESS IS WONDERFUL, BUT NOT IF IT CAUSES ME TO SLEEPWALK.
ARTEPHIUS, I MUST STOP TAKING THIS ELIXIR!
ARE YOU SURE? I COULD MAKE ANOTHER DOSE THAT STOPS YOU FROM SLEEPING ALTOGETHER! THAT WOULD STOP YOU FROM SLEEPWALKING, WOULDN'T IT?
HMMM...
WELL, THAT DOES SOUND INTRIGUING...
UH, PUSS? REMEMBER ALL THE MINOR CRIMES? DON'T DO IT.
I SHAN'T! ARTEPHIUS, DESTROY THE POTION!
SNIFF HMMM... SMELLS LIKE VITAMIN X!
LATER THAT DAY...
PEOPLE OF SAN LORENZO, I PROMISE YOU THAT I WILL CONTINUE TO BE HYPER-SUPER-AMAZINGLY VIGILANT...
BUT ONLY IN MODERATION.

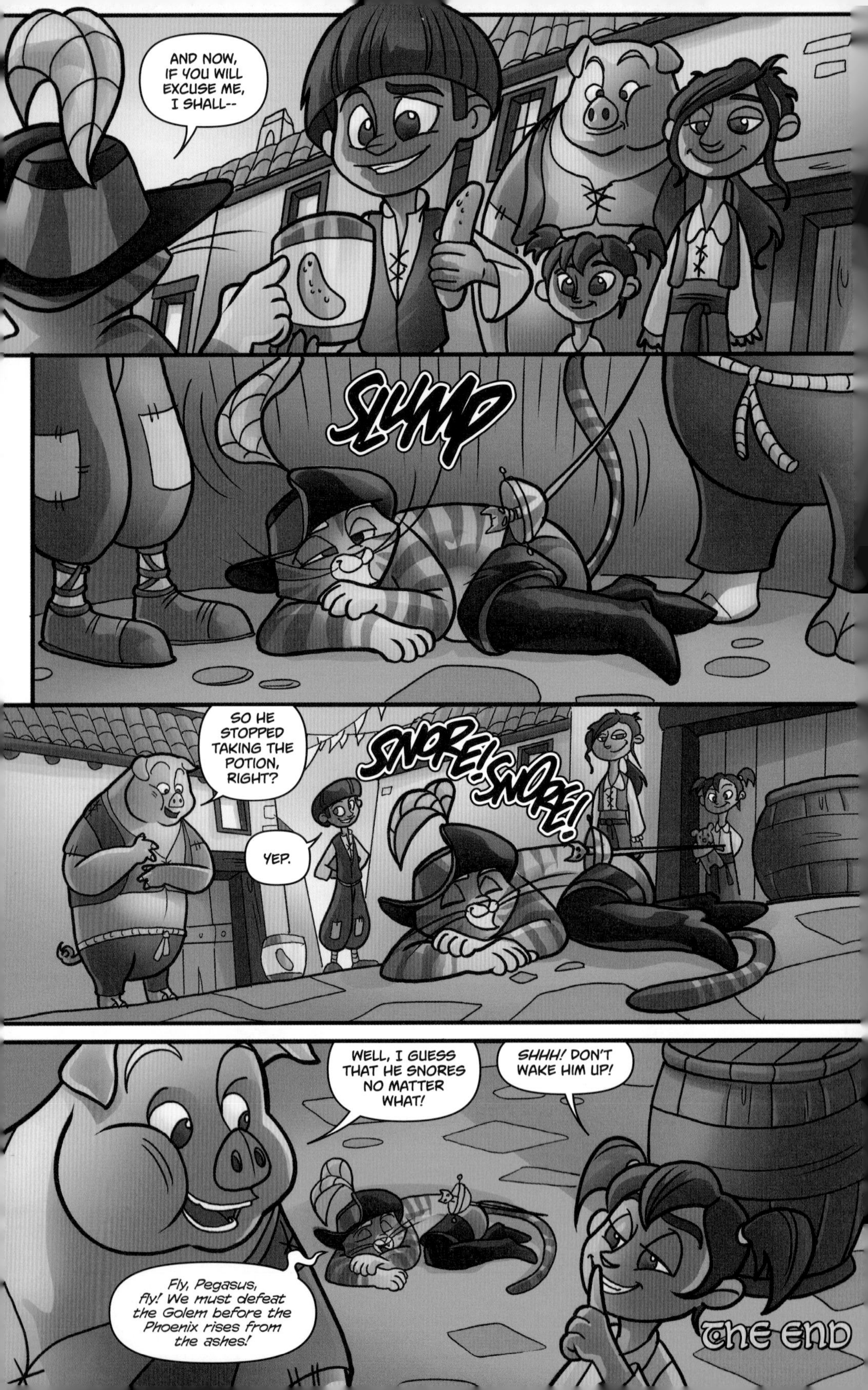
AND NOW, IF YOU WILL EXCUSE ME, I SHALL--
SLUMP
SO HE STOPPED TAKING THE POTION, RIGHT?
YEP.
SNORE! SNORE!
WELL, I GUESS THAT HE SNORES NO MATTER WHAT!
SHHH! DON'T WAKE HIM UP!
Fly, Pegasus, fly! We must defeat the Golem before the Phoenix rises from the ashes!
THE END

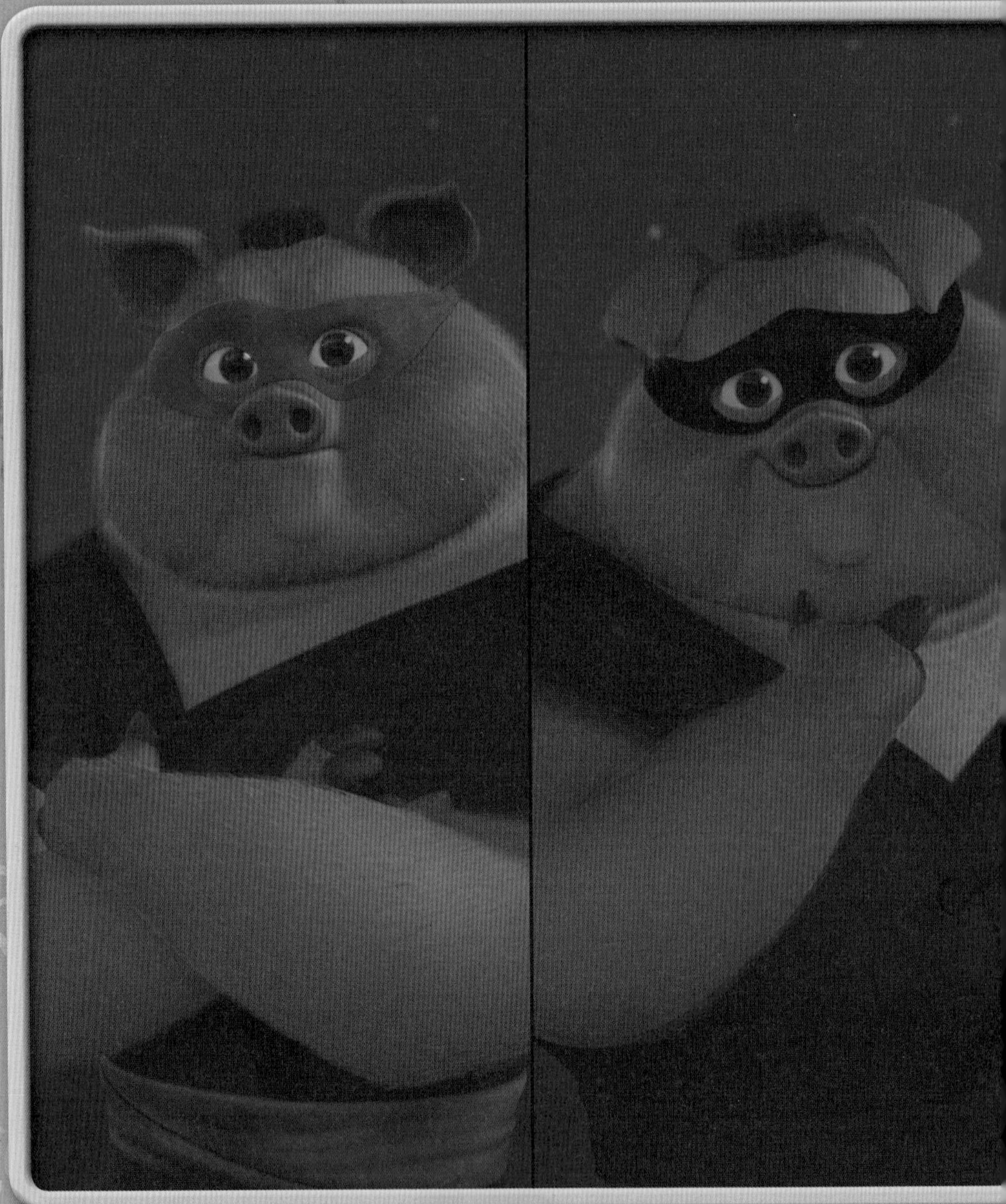

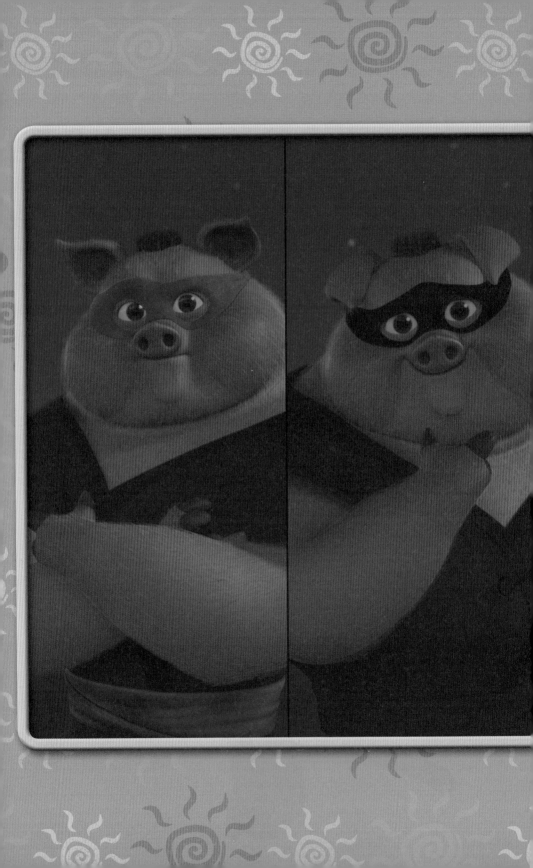

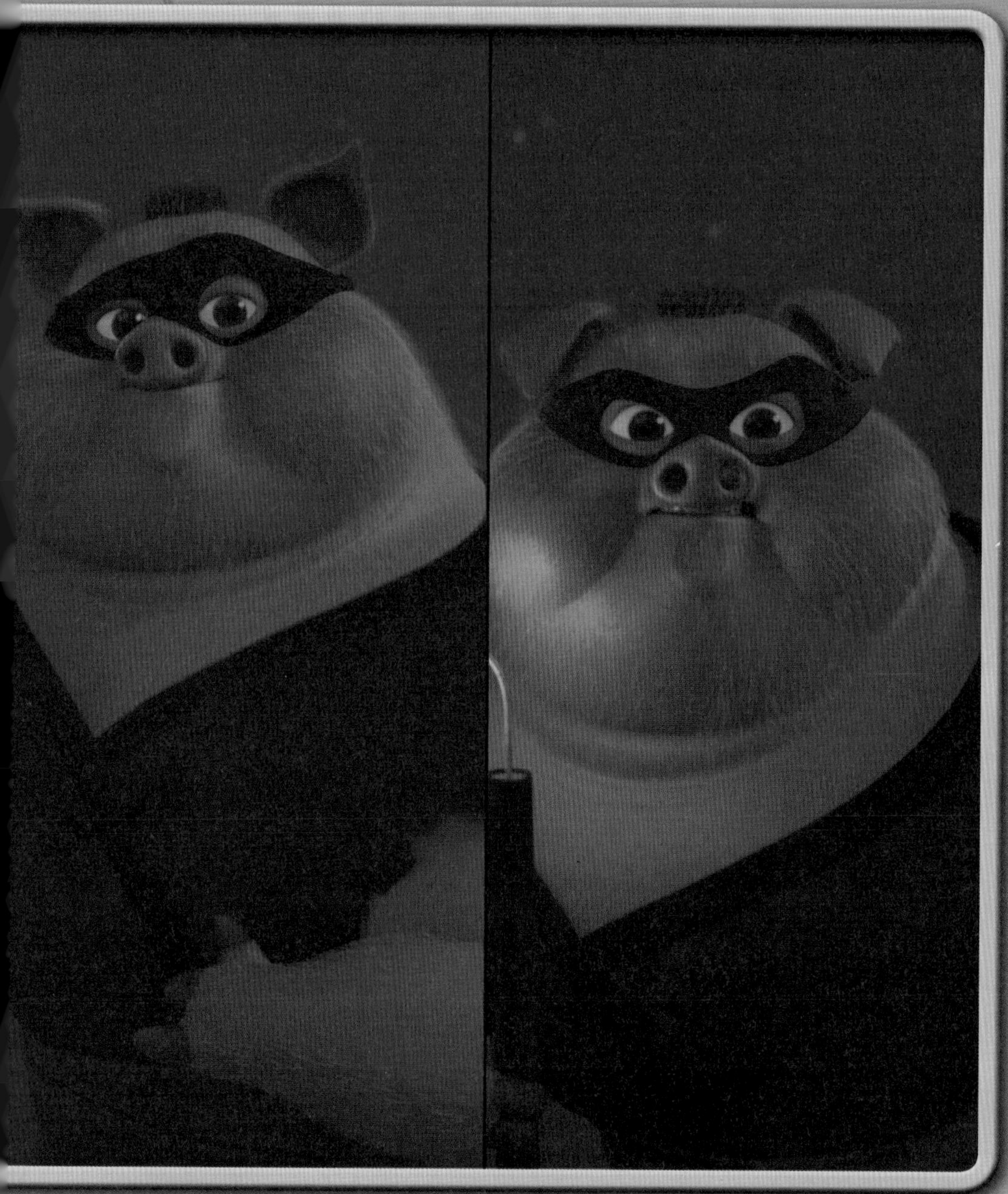

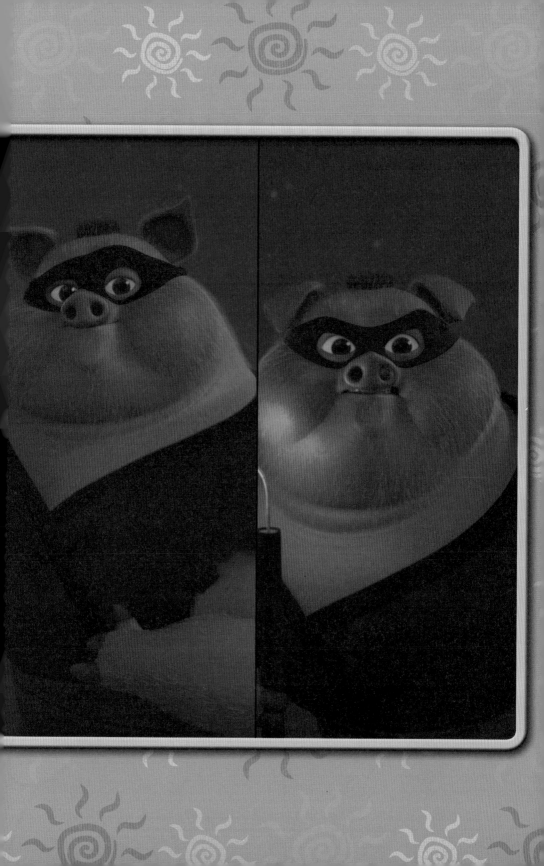

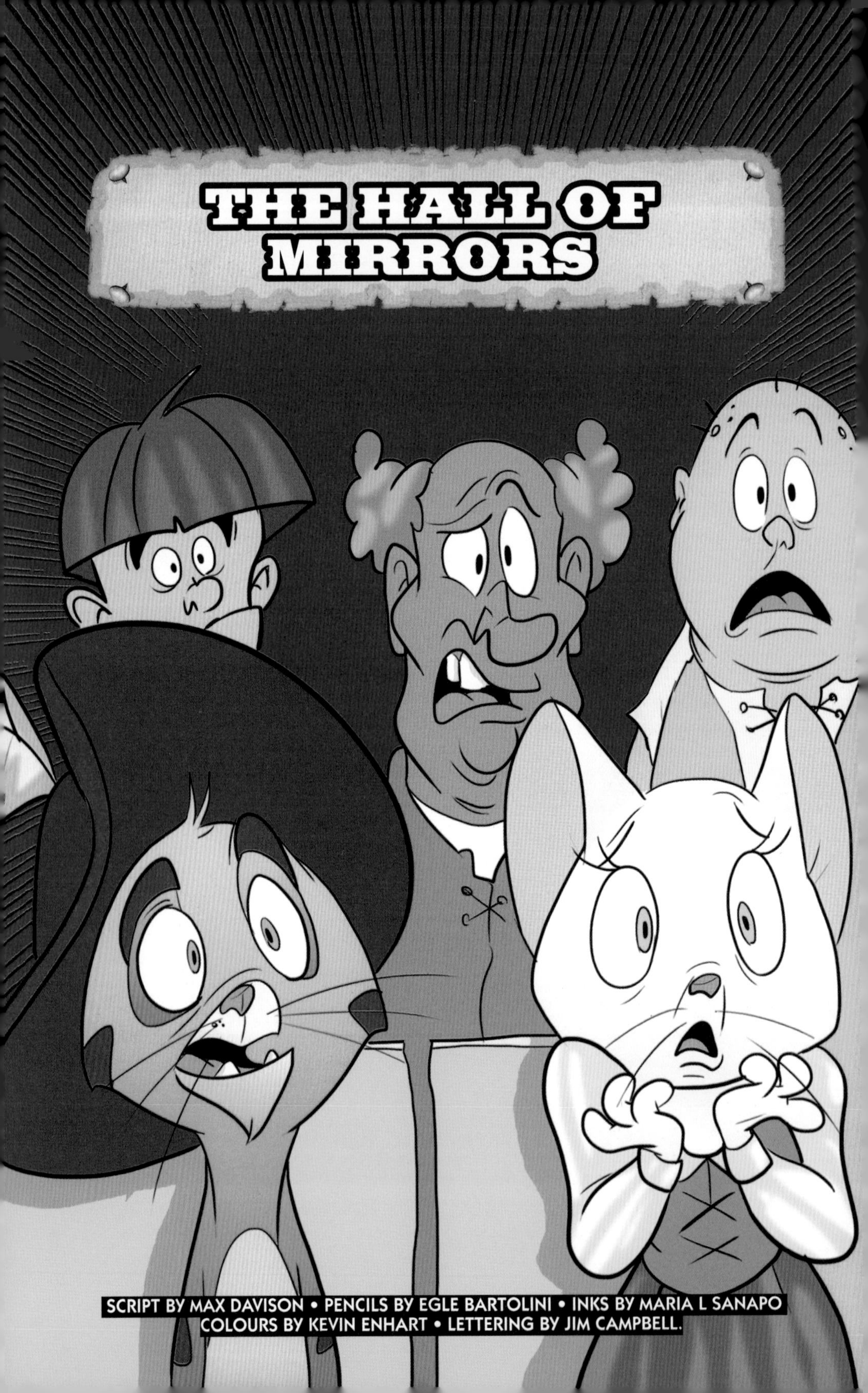
THE HALL OF MIRRORS
SCRIPT BY MAX DAVISON • PENCILS BY EGLE BARTOLINI • INKS BY MARIA L SANAPO
COLOURS BY KEVIN ENHART • LETTERING BY JIM CAMPBELL.

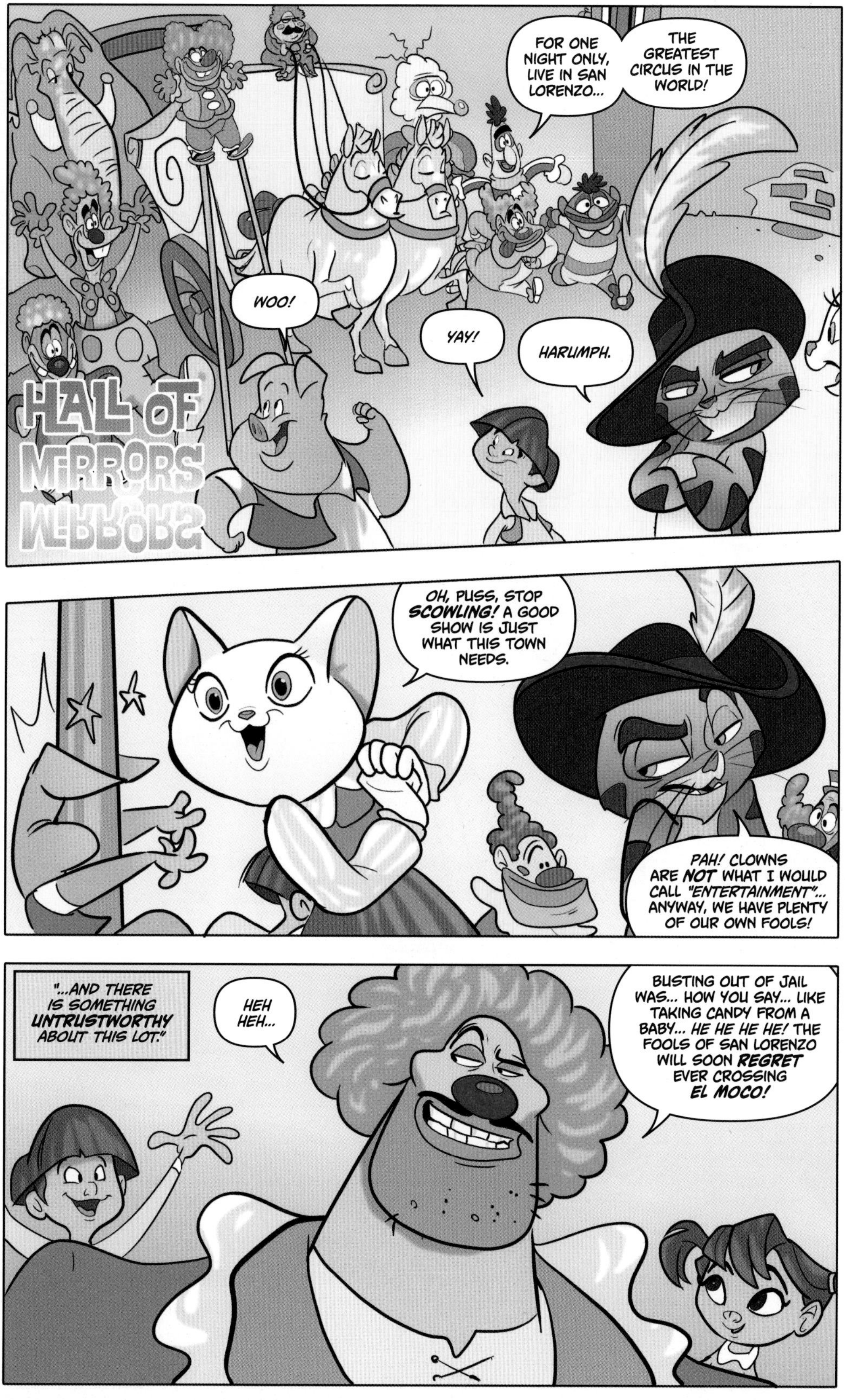
FOR ONE NIGHT ONLY, LIVE IN SAN LORENZO...
THE GREATEST CIRCUS IN THE WORLD!
WOO!
YAY!
HARUMPH.
HALL OF MIRRORS
OH, PUSS, STOP SCOWLING! A GOOD SHOW IS JUST WHAT THIS TOWN NEEDS.
PAH! CLOWNS ARE NOT WHAT I WOULD CALL "ENTERTAINMENT"... ANYWAY, WE HAVE PLENTY OF OUR OWN FOOLS!
"...AND THERE IS SOMETHING UNTRUSTWORTHY ABOUT THIS LOT."
HEH HEH...
BUSTING OUT OF JAIL WAS... HOW YOU SAY... LIKE TAKING CANDY FROM A BABY... HE HE HE HE! THE FOOLS OF SAN LORENZO WILL SOON REGRET EVER CROSSING EL MOCO!

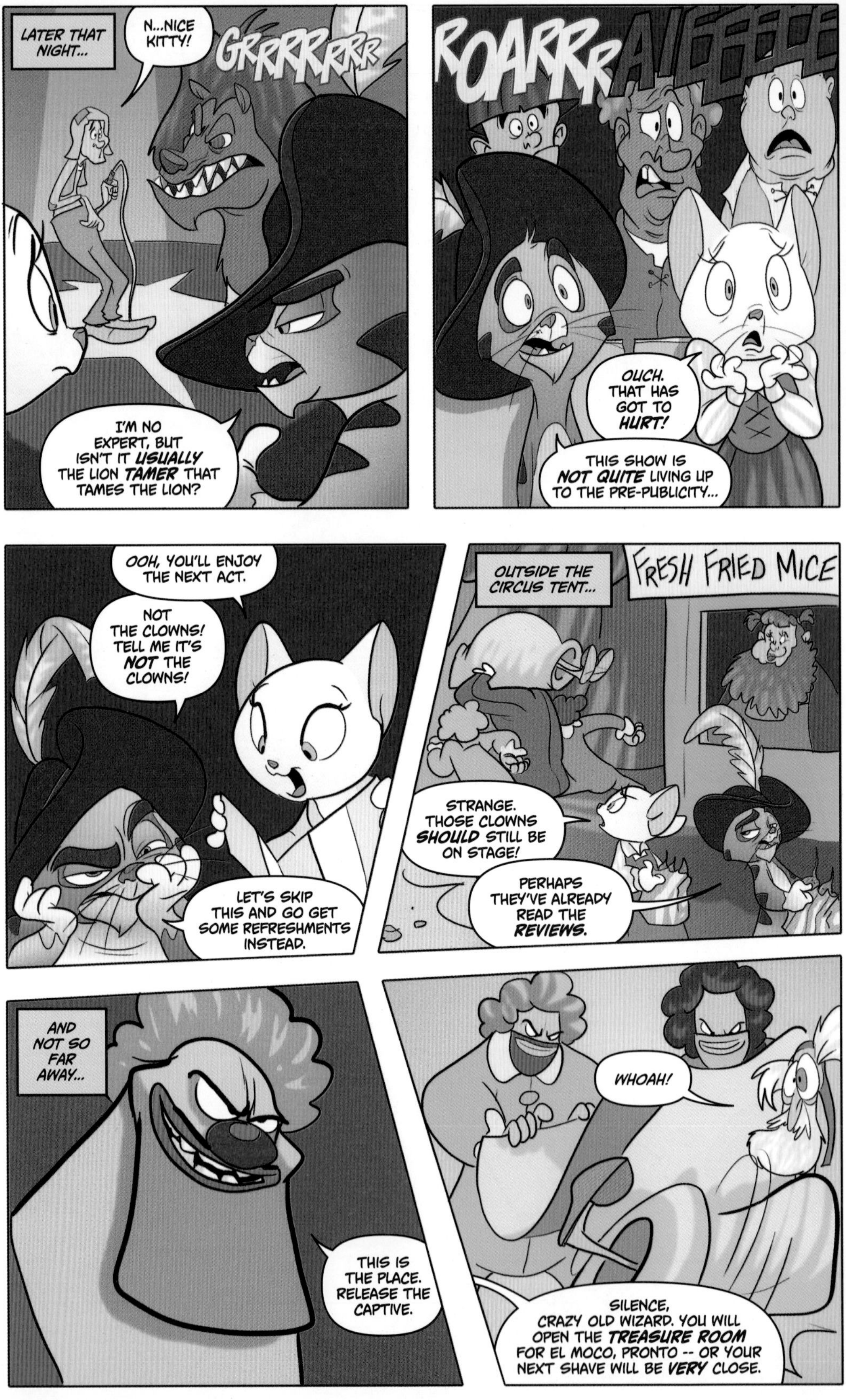
LATER THAT NIGHT...
N...NICE KITTY!
GRRRRRRRR
I'M NO EXPERT, BUT ISN'T IT USUALLY THE LION TAMER THAT TAMES THE LION?
ROARRR
AIEEEEEE
OUCH. THAT HAS GOT TO HURT!
THIS SHOW IS NOT QUITE LIVING UP TO THE PRE-PUBLICITY...
OOH, YOU'LL ENJOY THE NEXT ACT.
NOT THE CLOWNS! TELL ME IT'S NOT THE CLOWNS!
LET'S SKIP THIS AND GO GET SOME REFRESHMENTS INSTEAD.
OUTSIDE THE CIRCUS TENT...
FRESH FRIED MICE
STRANGE. THOSE CLOWNS SHOULD STILL BE ON STAGE!
PERHAPS THEY'VE ALREADY READ THE REVIEWS.
AND NOT SO FAR AWAY...
THIS IS THE PLACE. RELEASE THE CAPTIVE.
WHOAH!
SILENCE, CRAZY OLD WIZARD. YOU WILL OPEN THE TREASURE ROOM FOR EL MOCO, PRONTO -- OR YOUR NEXT SHAVE WILL BE VERY CLOSE.

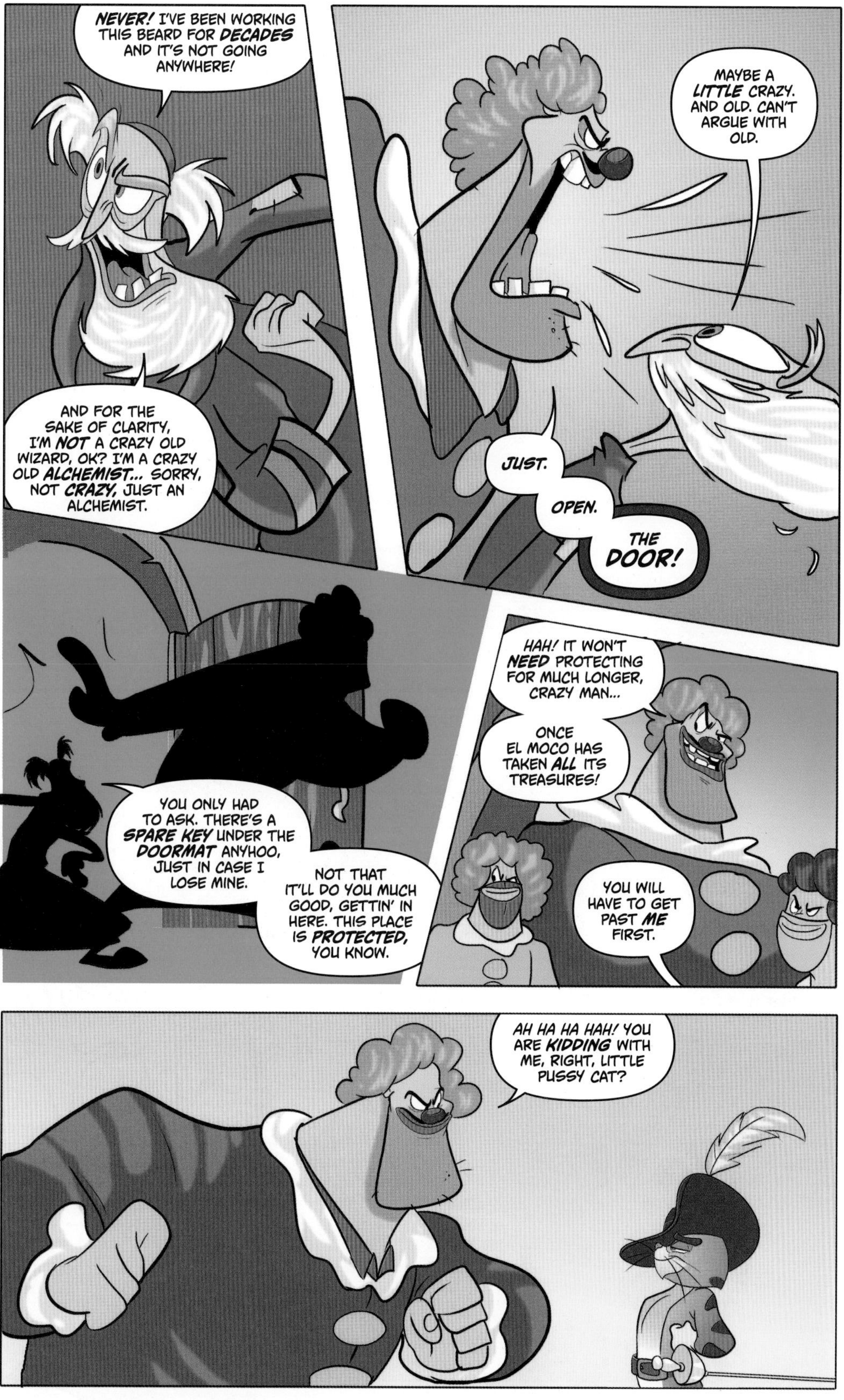
NEVER! I'VE BEEN WORKING THIS BEARD FOR DECADES AND IT'S NOT GOING ANYWHERE!
AND FOR THE SAKE OF CLARITY, I'M NOT A CRAZY OLD WIZARD, OK? I'M A CRAZY OLD ALCHEMIST... SORRY, NOT CRAZY, JUST AN ALCHEMIST.
MAYBE A LITTLE CRAZY. AND OLD. CAN'T ARGUE WITH OLD.
JUST.
OPEN.
THE DOOR!
YOU ONLY HAD TO ASK. THERE'S A SPARE KEY UNDER THE DOORMAT ANYHOO, JUST IN CASE I LOSE MINE.
NOT THAT IT'LL DO YOU MUCH GOOD, GETTIN' IN HERE. THIS PLACE IS PROTECTED, YOU KNOW.
HAH! IT WON'T NEED PROTECTING FOR MUCH LONGER, CRAZY MAN...
ONCE EL MOCO HAS TAKEN ALL ITS TREASURES!
YOU WILL HAVE TO GET PAST ME FIRST.
AH HA HA HAH! YOU ARE KIDDING WITH ME, RIGHT, LITTLE PUSSY CAT?

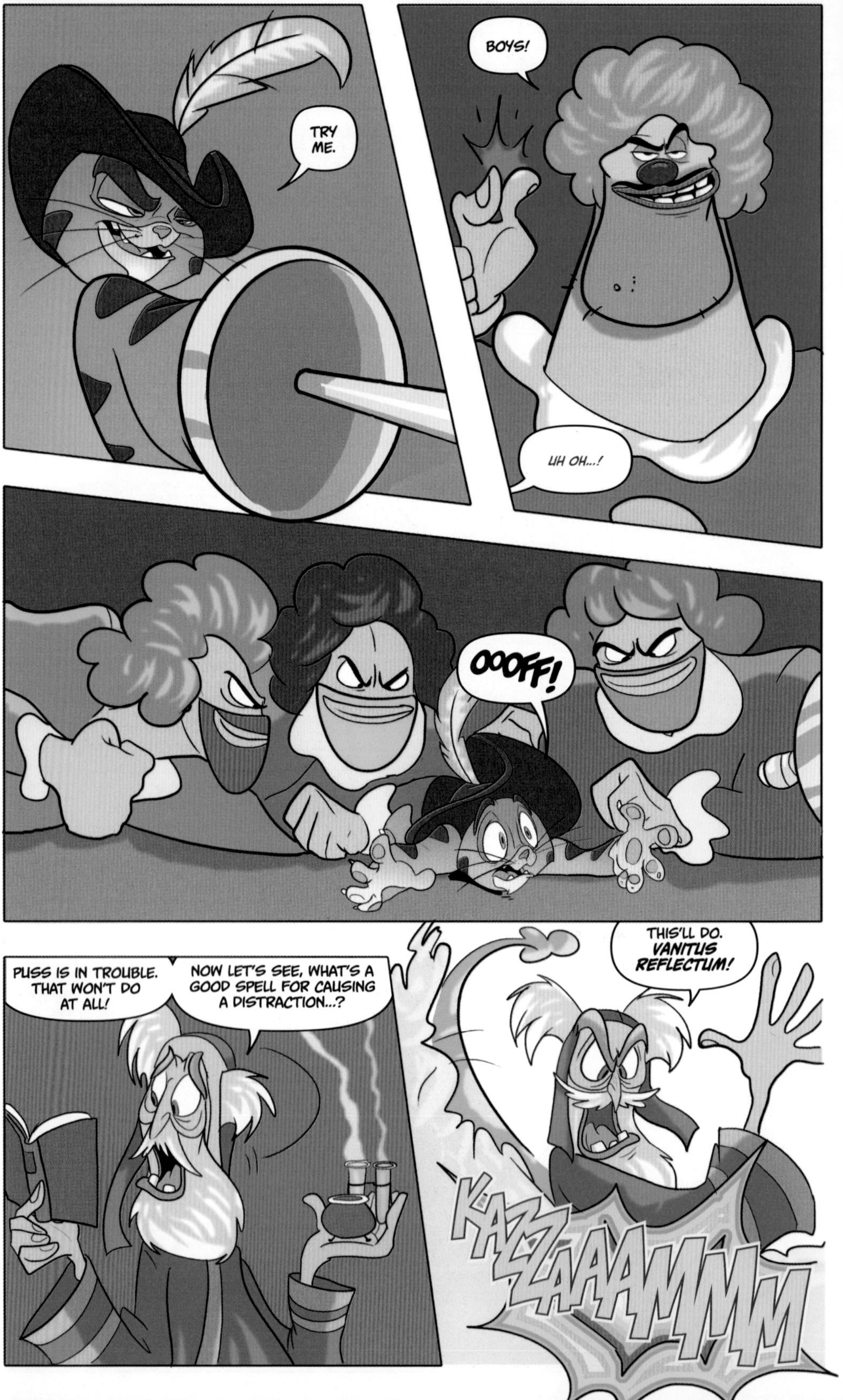
TRY ME.
BOYS!
UH OH...!
OOOFF!
PUSS IS IN TROUBLE. THAT WON'T DO AT ALL!
NOW LET'S SEE, WHAT'S A GOOD SPELL FOR CAUSING A DISTRACTION...?
THIS'LL DO. VANITUS REFLECTUM!
KAZZAAAMMMM

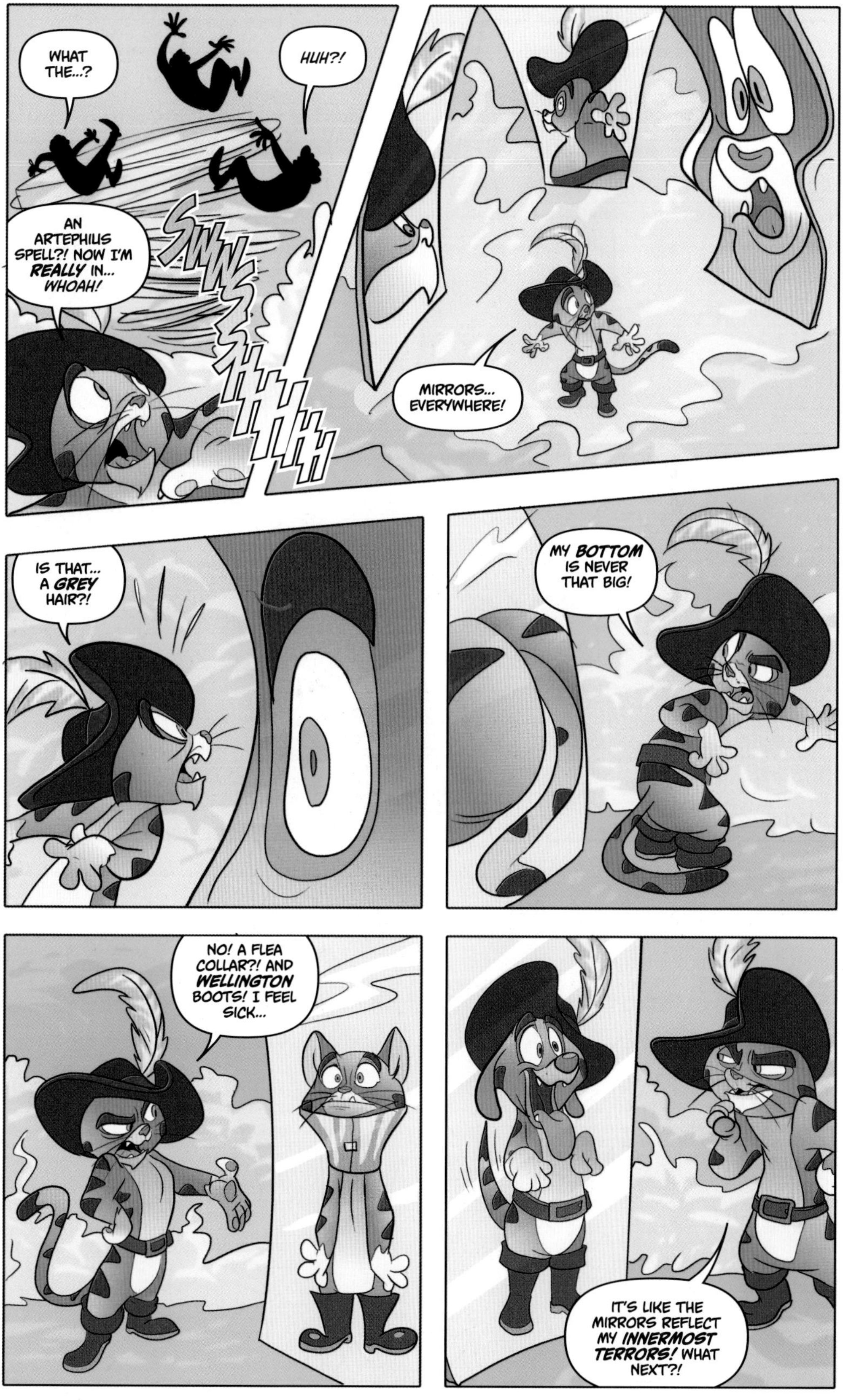
WHAT THE...?
HUH?!
AN ARTEPHIUS SPELL?! NOW I'M **REALLY** IN... **WHOAH!**
SWWSSHHHHH
MIRRORS... EVERYWHERE!
IS THAT... A **GREY** HAIR?!
MY **BOTTOM** IS NEVER THAT BIG!
NO! A FLEA COLLAR?! AND **WELLINGTON** BOOTS! I FEEL SICK...
IT'S LIKE THE MIRRORS REFLECT MY **INNERMOST TERRORS!** WHAT NEXT?!

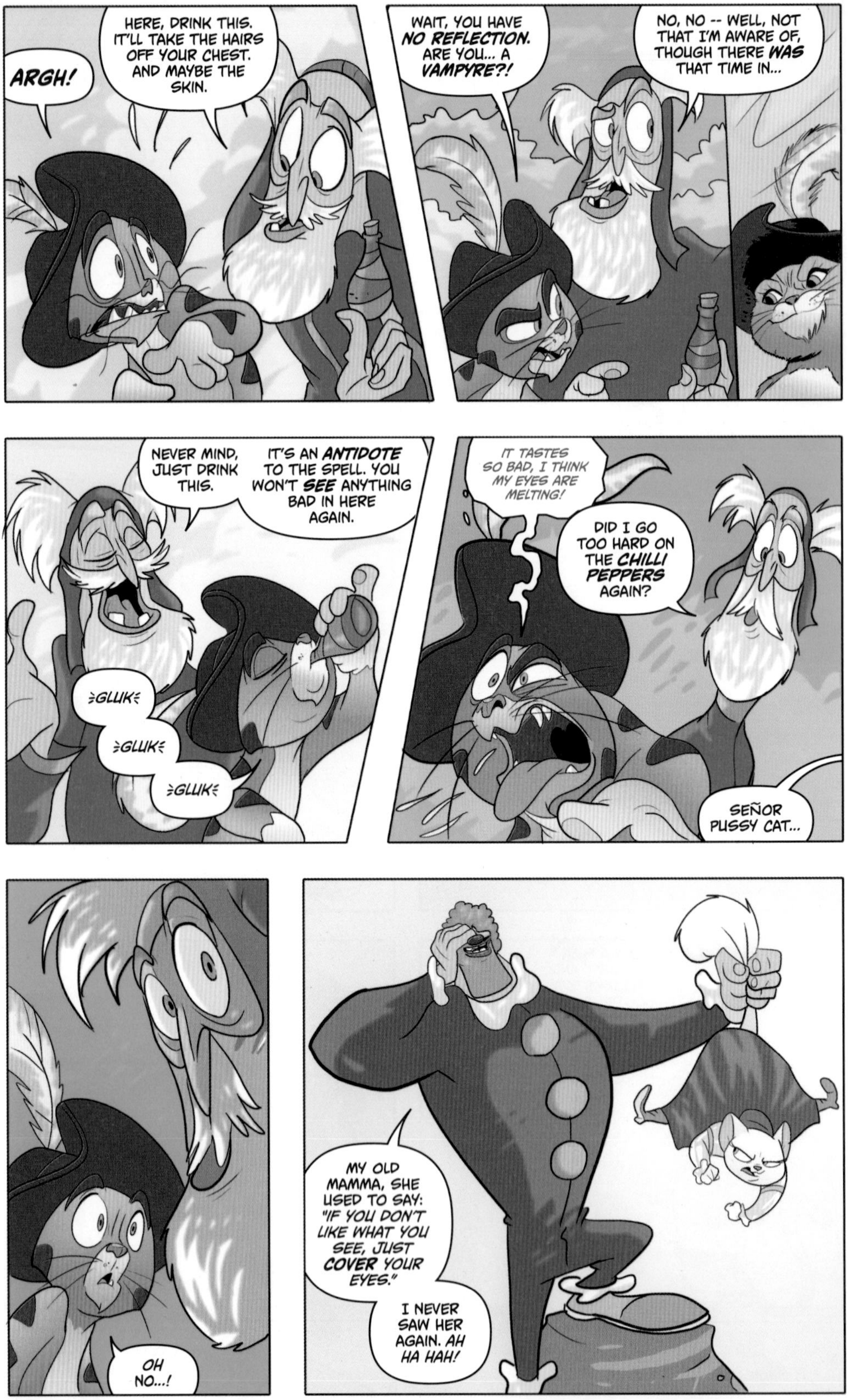
ARGH!
HERE, DRINK THIS. IT'LL TAKE THE HAIRS OFF YOUR CHEST. AND MAYBE THE SKIN.
WAIT, YOU HAVE NO REFLECTION. ARE YOU... A VAMPYRE?!
NO, NO -- WELL, NOT THAT I'M AWARE OF, THOUGH THERE WAS THAT TIME IN...
NEVER MIND, JUST DRINK THIS.
IT'S AN ANTIDOTE TO THE SPELL. YOU WON'T SEE ANYTHING BAD IN HERE AGAIN.
GLUK
GLUK
GLUK
IT TASTES SO BAD, I THINK MY EYES ARE MELTING!
DID I GO TOO HARD ON THE CHILLI PEPPERS AGAIN?
SEÑOR PUSSY CAT...
OH NO...!
MY OLD MAMMA, SHE USED TO SAY: "IF YOU DON'T LIKE WHAT YOU SEE, JUST COVER YOUR EYES."
I NEVER SAW HER AGAIN. AH HA HAH!

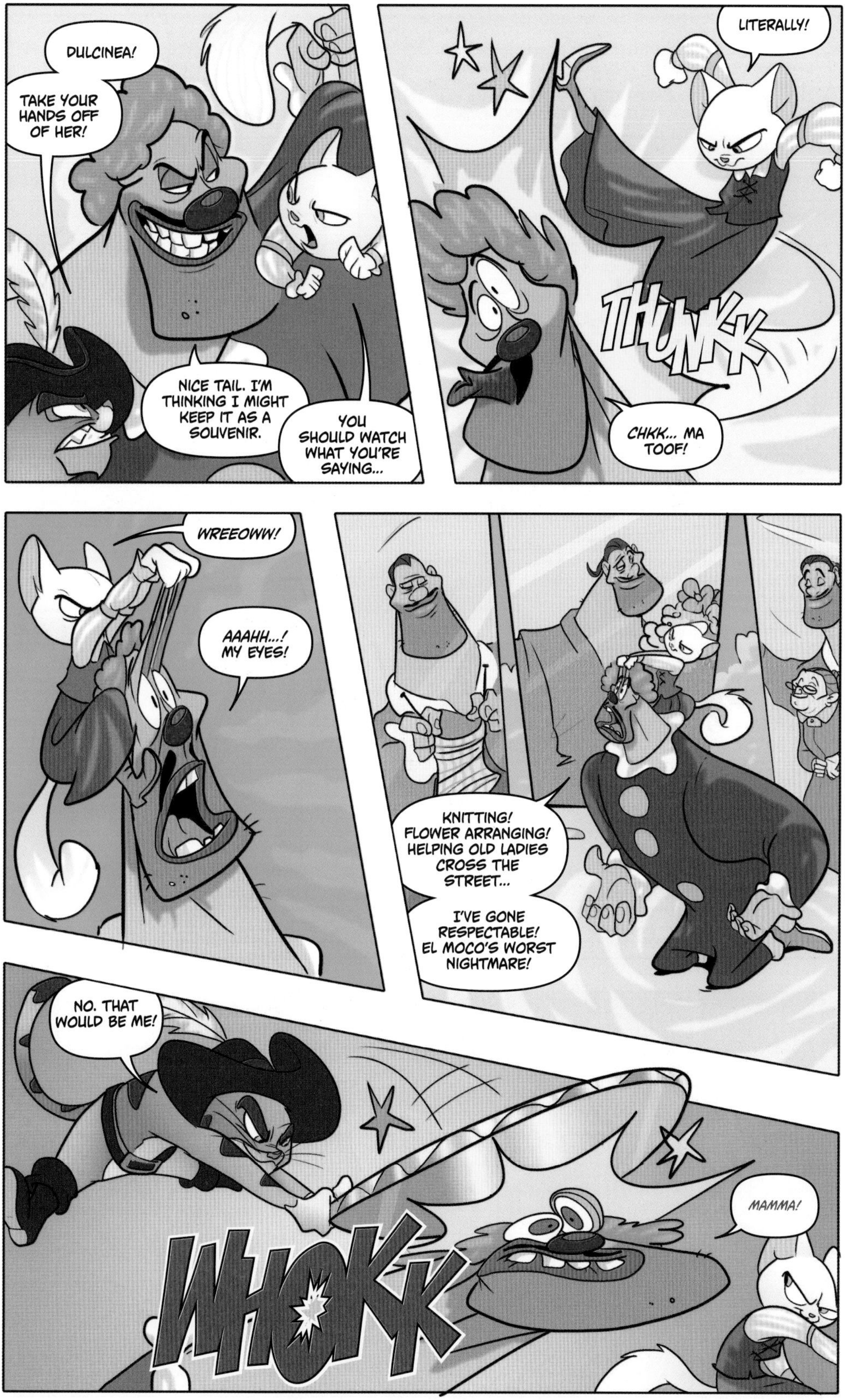
DULCINEA!
TAKE YOUR HANDS OFF OF HER!
NICE TAIL. I'M THINKING I MIGHT KEEP IT AS A SOUVENIR.
YOU SHOULD WATCH WHAT YOU'RE SAYING...
LITERALLY!
THUNKK
CHKK... MA TOOF!
WREEOWW!
AAAHH...! MY EYES!
KNITTING! FLOWER ARRANGING! HELPING OLD LADIES CROSS THE STREET...
I'VE GONE RESPECTABLE! EL MOCO'S WORST NIGHTMARE!
NO. THAT WOULD BE ME!
MAMMA!
WHOKK

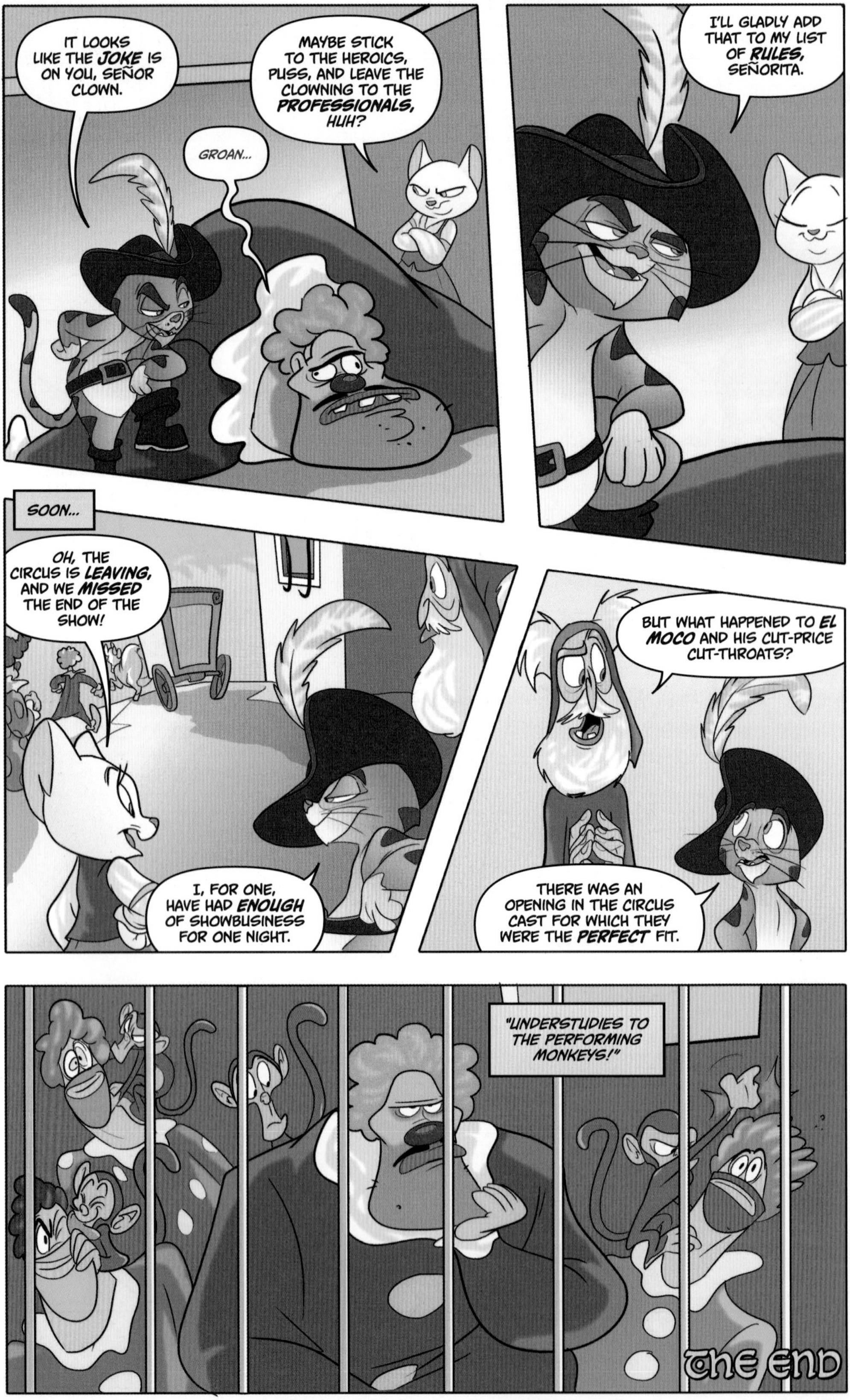
IT LOOKS LIKE THE JOKE IS ON YOU, SEÑOR CLOWN.
MAYBE STICK TO THE HEROICS, PUSS, AND LEAVE THE CLOWNING TO THE PROFESSIONALS, HUH?
GROAN...
I'LL GLADLY ADD THAT TO MY LIST OF RULES, SEÑORITA.
SOON...
OH, THE CIRCUS IS LEAVING, AND WE MISSED THE END OF THE SHOW!
I, FOR ONE, HAVE HAD ENOUGH OF SHOWBUSINESS FOR ONE NIGHT.
BUT WHAT HAPPENED TO EL MOCO AND HIS CUT-PRICE CUT-THROATS?
THERE WAS AN OPENING IN THE CIRCUS CAST FOR WHICH THEY WERE THE PERFECT FIT.
"UNDERSTUDIES TO THE PERFORMING MONKEYS!"
THE END

TITAN COMICS DIGESTS

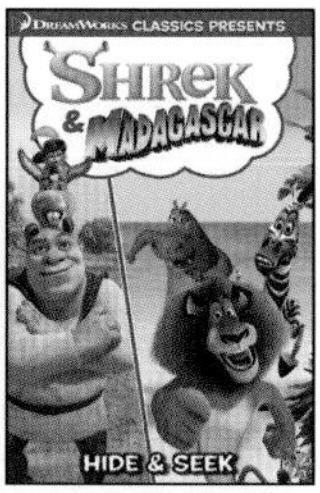
DreamWorks Classics Presents
Shrek & Madagascar
Hide & Seek

Dreamworks Classics – 'Hide & Seek'

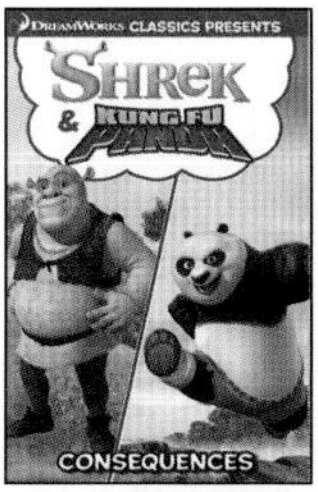
DreamWorks Classics Presents
Shrek & Kung Fu Panda
Consequences

Dreamworks Classics – 'Consequences'

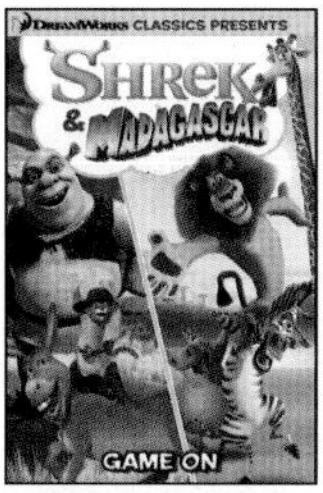
DreamWorks Classics Presents
Shrek & Madagascar
Game On

Dreamworks Classics – 'Game On'

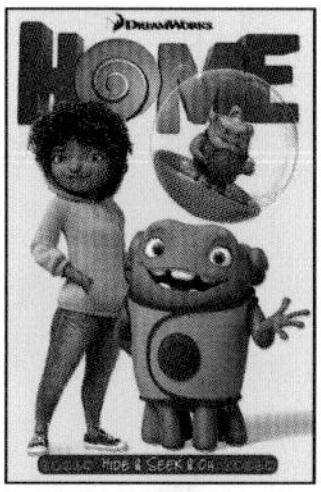
DreamWorks
Home

Dreamworks Home – Hide & Seek & Oh

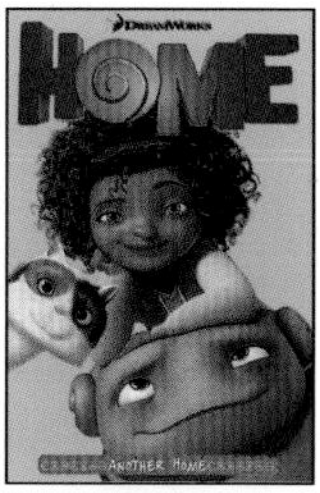
DreamWorks
Home

Dreamworks Home – Another Home

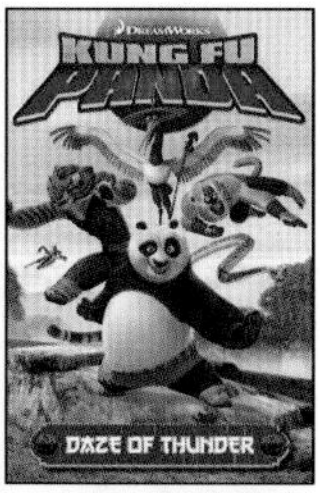
DreamWorks
Kung Fu Panda
Daze of Thunder

Kung Fu Panda – Daze of Thunder

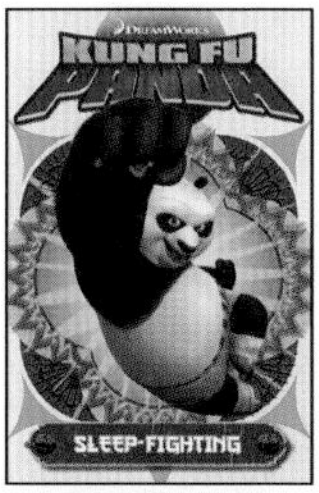
DreamWorks
Kung Fu Panda
Sleep-Fighting

Kung Fu Panda – Sleep-Fighting

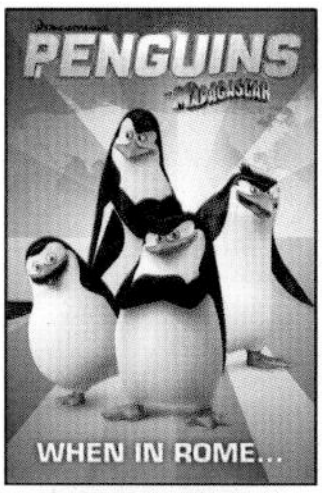
Penguins
of Madagascar
When in Rome...

Penguins of Madagascar – When in Rome...

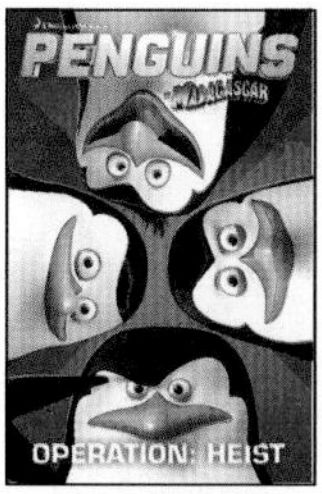
Penguins
of Madagascar
Operation: Heist

Penguins of Madagascar – Operation: Heist

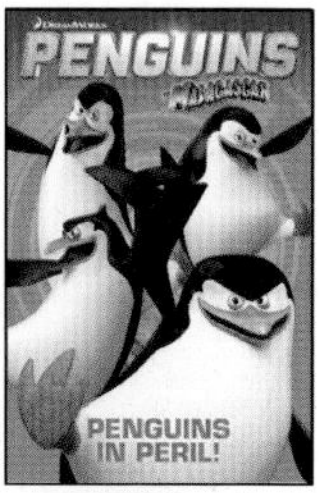
Penguins
of Madagascar
Penguins in Peril!

Penguins of Madagascar – Penguins in Peril

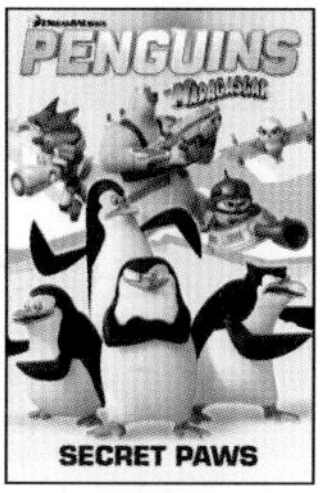
Penguins
of Madagascar
Secret Paws

Penguins of Madagascar – Secret Paws

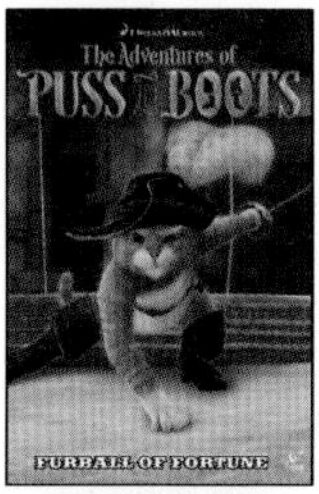
The Adventures of
Puss in Boots
Furball of Fortune

The Adventures of Puss In Boots – Furball of Fortune

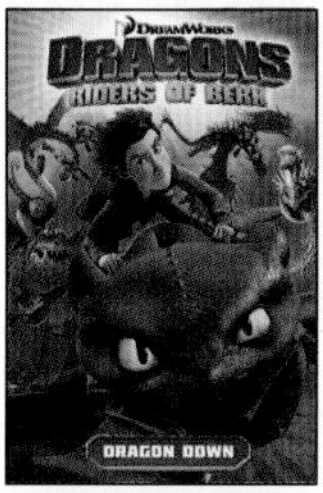
DreamWorks
Dragons
Riders of Berk
Dragon Down

DreamWorks Dragons: Riders of Berk – Dragon Down

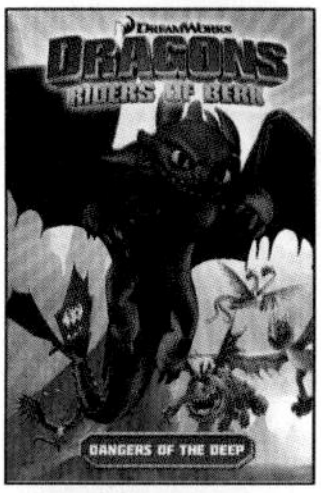
DreamWorks
Dragons
Riders of Berk
Dangers of the Deep

DreamWorks Dragons: Riders of Berk – Dangers of the Deep

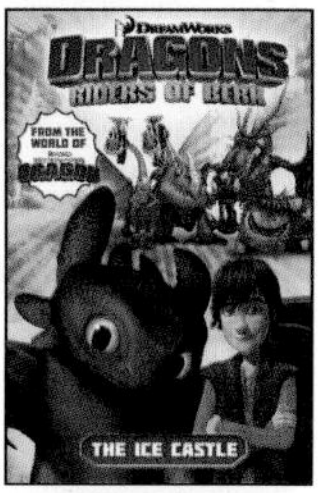
DreamWorks
Dragons
Riders of Berk
The Ice Castle

DreamWorks Dragons: Riders of Berk – The Ice Castle

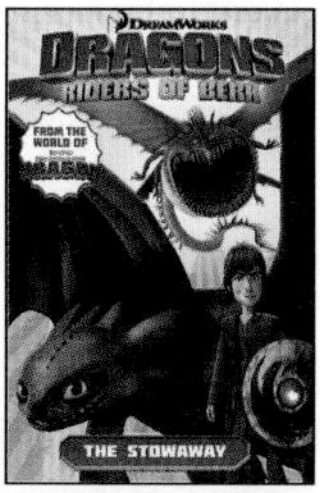
DreamWorks
Dragons
Riders of Berk
The Stowaway

DreamWorks Dragons: Riders of Berk – The Stowaway

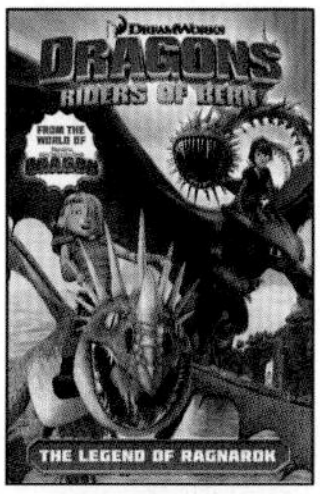
DreamWorks
Dragons
Riders of Berk
The Legend of Ragnarok

DreamWorks Dragons: Riders of Berk – The Legend of Ragnarok

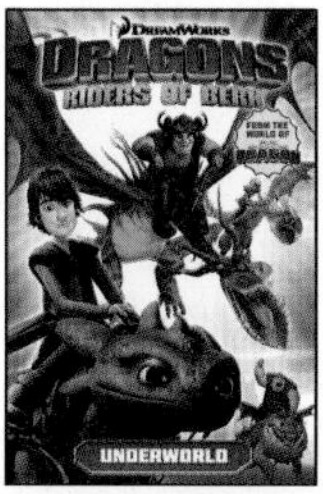
DreamWorks
Dragons
Riders of Berk
Underworld

DreamWorks Dragons: Riders of Berk – Underworld

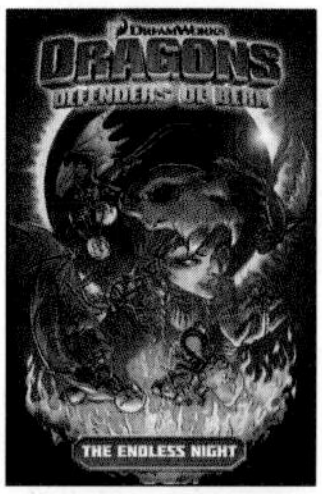
DreamWorks
Dragons
Defenders of Berk
The Endless Night

DreamWorks Dragons: Defenders of Berk - The Endless Night

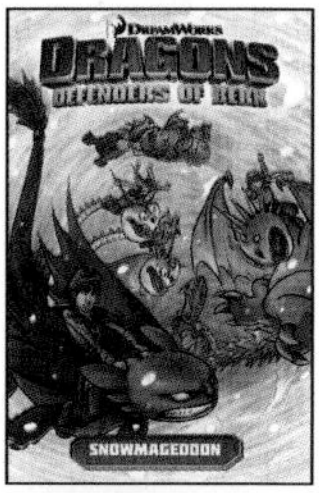
DreamWorks
Dragons
Defenders of Berk
Snowmageddon

DreamWorks Dragons: Defenders of Berk - Snowmageddon

TITAN COMICS

WWW.TITAN-COMICS.COM

ALSO AVAILABLE DIGITALLY

DreamWorks Animation SKG

TITAN COMICS GRAPHIC NOVELS

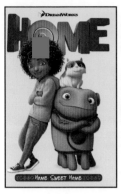

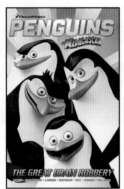

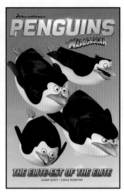

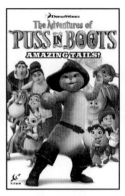

DreamWorks
HOME
HOME SWEET HOME

DREAMWORKS HOME: HOME SWEET HOME

DreamWorks
PENGUINS of MADAGASCAR
THE GREAT DRAIN ROBBERY

PENGUINS OF MADAGASCAR:
THE GREAT DRAIN ROBBERY

DreamWorks
PENGUINS of MADAGASCAR
THE ELITE-EST OF THE ELITE
CAVAN SCOTT • LUCAS PERREYRA

PENGUINS OF MADAGASCAR:
THE ELITE-EST OF THE ELITE

DreamWorks
The Adventures of
PUSS IN BOOTS
AMAZING TAILS!
TITAN

THE ADVENTURES OF PUSS IN BOOTS:
AMAZING TAILS

DreamWorks
KUNG FU PANDA
READY, SET, PO!

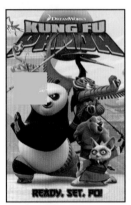

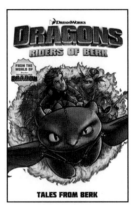

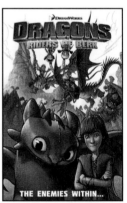

KUNG FU PANDA:
READY, SET, PO!

DreamWorks
DRAGONS
RIDERS OF BERK
TALES FROM BERK

DREAMWORKS DRAGONS:
RIDERS OF BERK – TALES FROM BERK

DreamWorks
DRAGONS
RIDERS OF BERK
THE ENEMIES WITHIN...

DREAMWORKS DRAGONS:
RIDERS OF BERK – THE ENEMIES WITHIN

DreamWorks
DRAGONS
RIDERS OF BERK
THE COLLECTORS EDITION

DREAMWORKS DRAGONS: RIDERS OF BERK
COLLECTORS EDITION

DreamWorks
DRAGONS
RIDERS OF BERK
MYTHS AND MYSTERIES

DREAMWORKS DRAGONS:
MYTHS AND MYSTERIES

DreamWorks
DRAGONS
DEFENDERS OF BERK
ICE AND FIRE

DREAMWORKS DRAGONS:
DEFENDERS OF BERK - ICE AND FIRE

TITAN COMICS

WWW.TITAN-COMICS.COM

ALSO AVAILABLE DIGITALLY

DREAMWORKS ANIMATION SKG

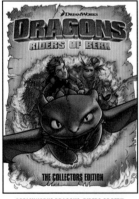

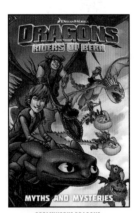

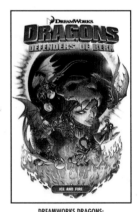

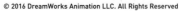

AVAILABLE SOON

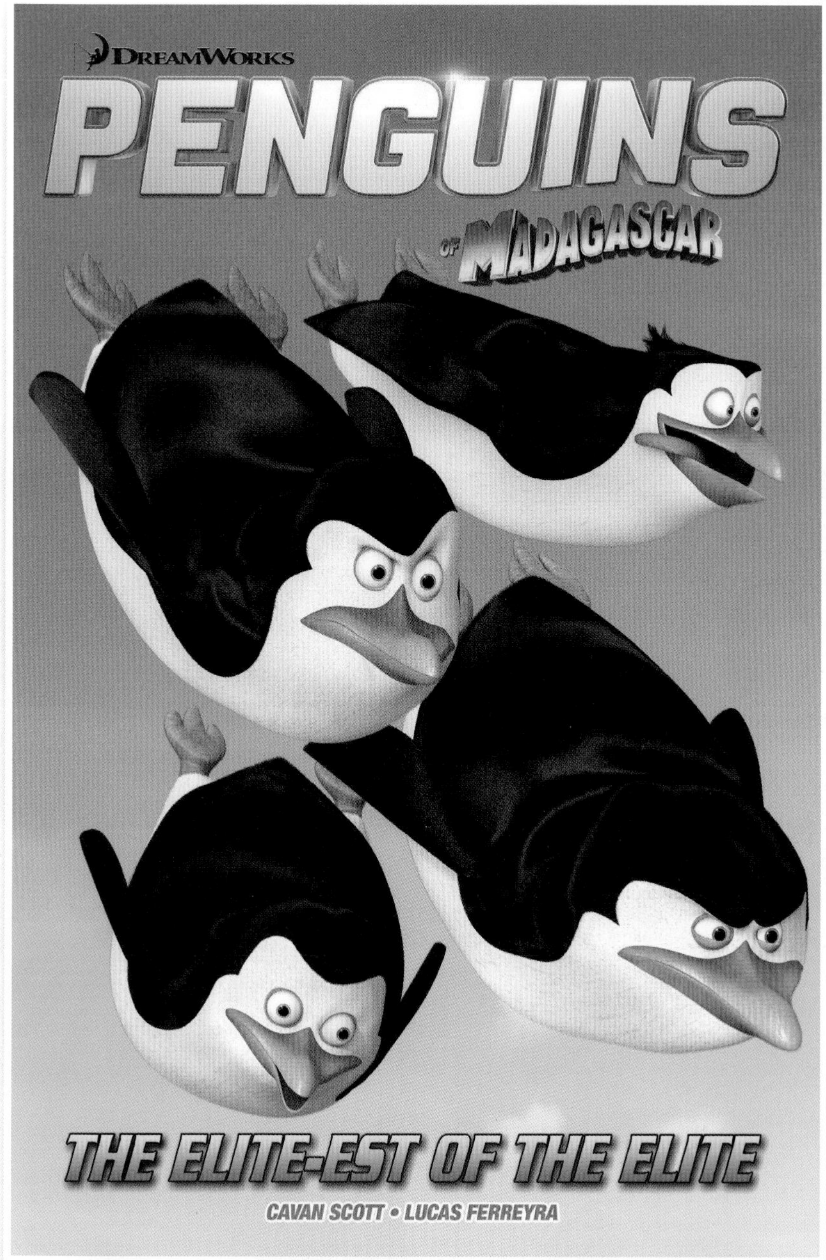
DreamWorks
PENGUINS
OF MADAGASCAR
THE ELITE-EST OF THE ELITE
CAVAN SCOTT • LUCAS FERREYRA

AN EPIC FOUR-PART STORY, PLUS BABY PENGUINS & NORTH WIND!

TITAN COMICS

WWW.TITAN-COMICS.COM

ALSO AVAILABLE DIGITALLY

DreamWorks Animation SKG

DreamWorks

The Adventures of PUSS IN BOOTS

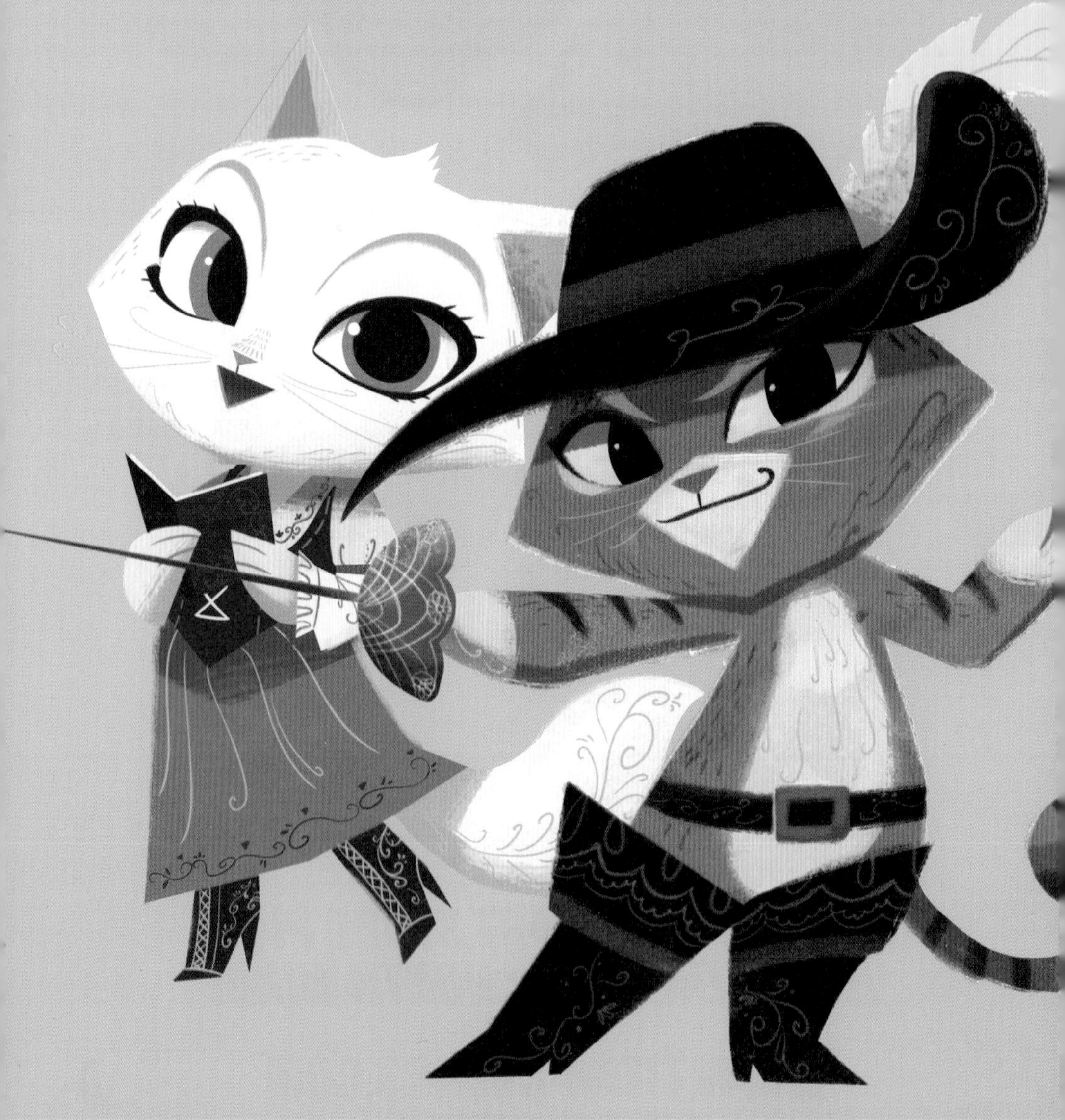